Meet the Capitol K-9 Unit officers and their loyal police dog partners

Officer: John Forrester

Age: 34

K-9 Partner: Samson the German Shepherd

Assignment: Protect his next-door neighbor from the person who keeps breaking into her newly inherited house.

Officer: Dylan Ralsey

Age: 32

K-9 Partner: Tico the Belgian Malinois

Assignment: Keep a diplomat's daughter safe from the man who killed her father.

Aside from her faith and her family, there's not much **Shirlee McCoy** enjoys more than a good book! When she's not teaching or chauffeuring her five kids, she can usually be found plotting her next Love Inspired Suspense story or wandering around the beautiful Inland Northwest in search of inspiration. Shirlee loves to hear from readers. Drop her a line at shirlee@shirleemccoy.com and visit her website at shirleemccoy.com.

Lenora Worth writes award-winning romance and romantic suspense. Three of her books finaled in the ACFW Carol Awards, and her Love Inspired Suspense novel *Body of Evidence* became a *New York Times* bestseller. Her novella in *Mistletoe Kisses* made her a *USA TODAY* bestselling author. With sixty books published and millions in print, she goes on adventures with her retired husband, Don, and enjoys reading, baking and shopping...especially shoe shopping.

CAPITOL
K-9 UNIT
CHRISTMAS

SHIRLEE McCOY
LENORA WORTH

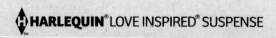
HARLEQUIN® LOVE INSPIRED® SUSPENSE

 LOVE INSPIRED BOOKS

ISBN-13: 978-0-373-44702-2

Capitol K-9 Unit Christmas

Copyright © 2015 by Harlequin Books S.A.

Thanks and acknowledgment to Shirlee McCoy and Lenora Worth
for their participation in the Capitol K-9 Unit series.

Protecting Virginia
Copyright © 2015 by Harlequin Books S.A.

Guarding Abigail
Copyright © 2015 by Harlequin Books S.A.

Recycling programs
for this product may
not exist in your area.

CONTENTS

PROTECTING VIRGINIA

Shirlee McCoy

To my Monday morning breakfast buddy.
Thanks for always making time for me, Ms. Marge!

You will keep in perfect peace all who trust in you,
all whose thoughts are fixed on you.
—Isaiah 26:3

ONE

The house looked exactly the way Virginia Johnson remembered it—a hulking Victorian with a wraparound porch and gingerbread trim. The once-lush lawn had died, the wrought iron fence that separated the yard from the sidewalk was leaning inward, but the ancient oak still stood at the right corner of the property, a tire swing hanging listlessly from its branches.

Even with dead grass and darkened windows, the property was impressive, the beautiful details of the house highlighted by bright winter sun. Most people would have been thrilled to inherit a place like this.

Virginia was horrified.

She walked up the driveway, her throat tight with a hundred memories that she'd rather forget, her hand clamped around the key that had come in the mail three weeks ago. It had been in a package with a letter from a lawyer who'd been trying to reach her for two months, a check for more money than she knew what to do with and the deed to the house.

She hadn't wanted any of it.

She'd torn up the check, tossed the deed and the key in the trash. Would have gone on with her life and pretended her grandmother-in-law, Laurel, hadn't left her everything the Johnson family owned. Except that kids were nosy, and Virginia's job as assistant housemother at All Our Kids Foster Home meant that she lived and worked with children all the time.

Most days, she loved her job. The day little Tommy Benson had taken the letter, torn-up check, key and deed out of the trashcan and delivered them to Virginia's boss, Cassie McCord, Virginia found herself wishing that she worked in a tiny little cubicle in a sales department somewhere. Because Cassie wasn't one to let things go. She couldn't understand why Virginia would let a beautiful home rot.

If you don't want it, why not sell it? she'd asked. *You haven't had any time off in three years. Take a couple of weeks off, contact an auction house. Have them auction what you don't want to keep, then you can put the house on the market. Imagine what you could do with the money, how many kids you could help.*

The last part had been the catalyst that had changed Virginia's mind. She *could* do a lot with the money from the estate. She could open another foster home. She could help hundreds of children.

And maybe…just maybe…going back to the place where she'd nearly died, the place where every one of her dreams had turned into a nightmare, would help her conquer the anxiety and fear that seemed to have taken over her life.

If it didn't kill her first.

She shivered, the late November air cutting through her coat and chilling her to the bone. Her legs felt stiff as she walked up the porch steps. It had been eight years since she'd seen the property, but it hadn't changed much. The door was still brick red, the porch and railing crisp white. The flowered welcome mat had been replaced by a plain black one. If she lifted it, would she see blood-stains on the porch boards?

She gagged at the thought, her hand shaking as she shoved the key in the lock. The door swung open before she could turn the knob, and she jumped back, startled, afraid.

Of what? her rational self whispered. *He's not here. Won't ever be here again.*

She stepped inside, closed the door behind her, stood there in the foyer the way she had the very first time she'd seen the property. Kevin had been beside her, proud of what he had to offer the woman he'd said he loved.

She gagged again, the scent of blood filling her nose. Only there was no blood. Not on the foyer floor. Not on the cream-colored walls. Someone had washed things down, painted them over, hidden the horror that had happened in a house that should have been filled with love.

"Just get it over with," she muttered, forcing herself to walk down the long hall and into the kitchen. She'd start her itemized list there.

The house had been in the Johnson family for five generations. It was filled to the brim with things that had been passed down from one family member to the next. The line had ended with Kevin's death. There were probably cousins of cousins somewhere, and Virginia wished her grandmother-in-law had found one of them to hand the property and the money over to. Instead, Laurel had passed the property on to Virginia. A guilt offering? It didn't matter. All Virginia wanted to do was get rid of it as quickly as possible.

A floorboard above her head creaked, and she froze, her hand on an old pitcher and bowl set that dated back to the nineteenth century.

"The house settling," she said aloud, the words echoing hollowly in the quiet room.

She knew the old house well, had lived in it for two long years. It creaked. It groaned. It protested its age loudly. Especially in the winter. She knew it, but she was still terrified, her hand shaking as she set the pitcher down.

The floor creaked again, and every fear that haunted her dreams, every terror that woke her from sound sleep, filled her mind. She inhaled. Exhaled. Told herself that she had nothing to be afraid of.

Another board creaked. It sounded like someone walking through the upstairs hallway, heading toward the servants' stairs. *The stairs that led straight down into the kitchen.*

The door to the stairwell was closed, the old crystal doorknob glinting in the overhead light. She cocked her head to the side and listened to what sounded like the landing at the top of the stairs groaning. Her imagination. It had to be.

She opened the door, because she was tired of always being afraid, always jumping at shadows, always panicking. The stairwell was narrow and dark, the air musty. She glanced up, expecting to see the other door, the one that led into the upstairs hallway.

A man stood on the landing. Tall. Gaunt. Hazel eyes and light brown hair.

"Kevin," she breathed, because he looked so much like her husband had that her heart nearly stopped.

He blinked, smiled a smile that made her skin crawl.

"Ginny," he murmured, and that was all she needed to hear.

She ran to the back door and fumbled with the bolt, sure she heard his footsteps on the stairs, his feet padding on the tile behind her.

She didn't look. Couldn't look.

The bolt slid free, and she yanked the door open, sprinted outside.

"Ginny!" the man called, as she jumped off the porch stairs and raced toward the back edge of the property. "Is this the way you treat a man who gave you everything?"

She screamed, the sound ripping from her throat, screaming again as footsteps pounded behind her.

She made it to the hedge that separated the Johnson property from the one behind it and plunged through winter-dry foliage, branches snagging her hair, ripping at her skin.

Was he behind her? His hand reaching to drag her back?

Impossible! Kevin had died eight years ago!

But someone was there, someone was following.

She shoved through the remainder of the hedge, ran into the open, and he was there. Standing in front of her, his broad form backlit by sunlight, his face hidden in shadows.

She pivoted away, screaming again and again.

He snagged her coat, pulled her backward, and she knew that every nightmare she'd ever had, every horrible memory she'd tried to forget had finally come for her.

The woman was hysterical. No doubt about that. Terrified, too. The last thing Capitol K-9 police officer John Forrester wanted to do was scare her more, but he couldn't let her go. She was obviously running from something or someone, and he didn't want her to run right back into whatever danger she'd fled.

"Calm down," he said, tugging her back another step. "I'm not going to hurt you."

She whirled around, took a swing at his head, her fist just missing his nose.

Beside him his K-9 partner, Samson, growled.

That seemed to get her attention.

She froze, her eyes wide as her gaze dropped to the German shepherd. Samson had subsided, his dark eyes locked on Virginia, his muscles relaxed. Obviously, he didn't see the woman as too much of a threat.

"He's not going to hurt you, either," John assured the woman.

She didn't look convinced, but she wasn't screaming any longer.

"That wasn't you in the house," she said as if that made perfect sense.

"What house?" he asked, eyeing the hedge she'd just torn through. The property on the other side of it had been empty for longer than John had been renting the Hendersons' garage apartment. According to his landlords, the elderly woman who owned the house had moved to an assisted-living facility over a year ago.

"Laurel's," the woman said, her hand trembling as she tucked a strand of light brown hair behind her ear. She looked vaguely familiar, her soft blue eyes sparking a memory that he couldn't quite catch hold of.

"Laurel is your friend?" he prodded, anxious to figure out what was going on and get back to his day off.

"My husband's grandmother. She left me the house, so I guess it's actually mine," she corrected herself.

"And you think someone was in there?"

"Someone *was* in there. I saw him."

"Your husband maybe?"

"My husband," she said, every word brittle and sharp, "is dead."

"I'm sorry."

She didn't respond, just fumbled in her pocket and pulled out a cell phone. "I need to call the police."

"I can check things out for you," he offered, because

he was there, and because if someone was in the house, the guy would be gone long before the police arrived.

"I don't think that would be safe," she said, worrying her lower lip, her finger hovering over the 9 on her phone. "He could have a weapon or—"

"I'm a police officer," he interrupted. "I work for Capitol K-9."

She looked up, her gaze sharp. "Then you know Gavin McCord."

The comment brought back the memory he'd been searching for. Captain Gavin McCord's wedding. His bride and her entourage of foster kids, the quiet woman who'd been with them. He hadn't paid all that much attention to her. She'd been pretty enough, her hair swept into some elaborate style, her dress understated, her shoes sturdy. Nothing showy about her. They might have been introduced. He couldn't remember. He'd been too busy thinking about getting food from the buffet.

"You're Cassie's friend," he said, pulling Samson's lead from his pocket and attaching it to the shepherd's collar.

"Yes. Virginia Johnson. Cassie and I work together at All Our Kids." She glanced at the hedge again, tucking another stray strand of hair behind her ear. Her nervous energy made him antsy. He didn't much like sitting idle when he could be doing something, and right at that moment, he and Samson could be searching for whomever she'd seen.

"Tell you what, Virginia," he said. "Go ahead and call the police while I look around. If there's someone in the house, we're giving him way too much time to get away."

"I hope he does get away," she muttered.

"You want him coming back?" he asked, and she flinched.

"No, but I don't want you killed, either, Officer—"

"John Forrester. Stay here. I'll be back soon."

"I'm not waiting out here by myself," she said, moving in behind him as he made his way to the shrubs.

"Then wait at my place." He shoved the keys into her hands, pointing her toward the external staircase that led to his second-floor garage apartment.

"But—"

"Find!" he said, commanding Samson to move forward.

The Shepherd took off, lunging through the shrubs and out into a pristine yard, nose to the ground, body relaxed. He was trained in apprehension and protection. He knew how to track a suspect, corner him and disarm him if necessary.

He was also good at sensing danger, at knowing when someone was around who didn't belong. Right now, he was focused on a scent trail. Probably Virginia's.

John followed as Samson beelined across the lawn and headed straight toward the large Victorian. The Shepherd bounded up the porch stairs, and stopped at a door. Cracked open, a little wedge of light visible beyond, it looked as if it opened into a kitchen.

"Hold!" he commanded and Samson settled onto his haunches, eyes trained on the door.

John nudged it open, peering into an empty kitchen.

"Find," he commanded, and Samson trotted into the room.

The house lay silent, the air thick with something that made the hair on the back of John's neck stand on end. He'd been in enough dangerous situations to know when he was walking into trouble. He could feel it like a cold breeze brushing against his skin.

Samson sensed it, too. His scruff bristled, his body language changing. No longer relaxed, he sniffed the air and moved toward a doorway to their left. Beyond it, a staircase wound its way to the second floor.

Samson charged up, his well-muscled body moving silently. John moved with him. In sync with the Shepherd's loping gait, muscles tense, every nerve alert, he jogged onto the second-floor landing and into a wide hallway. Seven doors. All closed. Another staircase that led downstairs.

Samson growled, the deep low warning seeming to echo through the hallway.

"Police!" John shouted. "Come on out or I'll send my dog to find you."

There was a flurry of movement below. Fabric rustling, footsteps pounding.

Samson barked, yanking at the lead, tugging John into a full-out run.

A door creaked open as they raced downstairs and into a large foyer.

The front door?

Samson veered away from it, pulling John through the foyer into an old-fashioned parlor.

Cold air filled the room, swirling in from an open door that emptied onto a wraparound porch.

"Find!" John commanded, and Samson raced through the open doorway and out into the crisp winter day, his well-muscled body tense with anticipation.

Someone had been in the house. There was no doubt about that. What he was doing there was something John had every intention of finding out.

He ran down porch steps, Samson bounding in front of him. No hesitation. The dog had the scent, and he'd follow it until they found their quarry. Once he did, the guy was going to be very sorry he'd picked that house.

TWO

Virginia didn't know what to do.

That was going to be a problem, because standing in the middle of some guy's yard, waiting while he searched her house for a dead man? That was nuts.

Yet that was exactly what Virginia was doing.

She'd called the police.

She knew they were on the way.

She could have gone inside the garage apartment like Officer Forrester had suggested, but she was frozen with fear, so afraid that she'd move the wrong way, head the wrong direction, make the wrong choice, that she wasn't doing anything at all.

"Snap out of it," she muttered, and the words seemed to break terror's hold.

She could breathe again, think again.

And what she was thinking was that she needed to meet the police and explain what she'd seen. Crazy as it might sound to them, Kevin had been in that house. Or someone who'd looked an awful lot like him, because there was no way the man could have actually been her husband. She'd seen Kevin's gravesite. She'd read the inscription that his grandmother had had carved on the marble stone: *Beloved son. Beloved husband.* Virginia had wanted to scratch those words out, just leave his birth and death dates.

Of course, she hadn't.

She'd always played by the rules, done what she was supposed to, tried to be the best that she could be. That included being a survivor. So, she'd done what the therapist had suggested—gone to the gravesite, read the police report, the coroner's report, the reports from the doctor who'd pronounced Kevin dead. She'd tried to heal, because that was what everyone had expected, and it was what she wanted to do.

Eight years later, she didn't know if she could heal from what she'd been through. The wounds had scarred over, but they weren't gone. They still throbbed and pulsed and ached every time something reminded her of Kevin.

Kevin, who apparently had a doppelgänger, one who knew who Virginia was and knew that Kevin had called her Ginny.

She shuddered.

Somewhere in the distance, a dog was barking. Officer Forrester's K-9 partner?

Maybe, and maybe they'd found the guy who'd been in the house. She knew enough about the Capitol K-9 Unit to know that every member was handpicked to do the job. They were all well trained, driven, hardworking. She'd seen that firsthand when one of the foster children she and Cassie were caring for had been in danger. The Capitol K-9 team had stepped in, protecting Cassie, Virginia and the kids.

Virginia had been more than happy to let them do it; but, then, she'd spent most of the past few years letting other people call the shots. It was so much easier to do that than to risk making a mistake, doing something that would get her into the kind of trouble she'd found her-self in with Kevin.

She needed to change that. She knew it. She'd known it for a long time. Accepting the inheritance from Lau-rel was part of that. Taking control of her life, being less afraid and more courageous—that was the other part.

Sirens were screaming, and she knew the police were close. She could keep standing where she was or she could head back to the house and wait for them to ar-rive. A few weeks ago, she would have stayed put, but she had plans. Big ones. She wanted to open her own foster home, take the money she'd inherited and put it to good use. She really felt as if that was what God wanted her to do, but there was no way she could until she started taking control again, started regaining what she'd lost eight years ago.

She took a deep breath, ignoring the sick feeling of dread in the pit of her stomach as she headed back across the yard.

She bypassed the house, keeping a good distance be-tween herself and the building. She didn't think the Kevin look-alike was still there. She'd heard Officer Forrester's dog howling, and she knew enough about K-9 work to know that meant he was on a scent.

She hated the house, though, and now she had new bad memories to add to the old ones.

A police cruiser was pulling into the driveway as she ran into the front yard. She waited, her heart pounding painfully as the officer climbed out. Midfifties with salt-and-pepper hair and a handlebar mustache that seemed out of place in Washington, DC, he had the rugged kind of hardness she'd noticed in the faces of a lot of veteran police officers.

"Ma'am?" he said. "Did you call about an intruder?"

"Yes." She moved toward him, her legs just a little shaky. She needed to get herself under control. The last thing she wanted was a full-blown panic attack. "He was in the house when I arrived."

"Is he still there?"

"I don't think so."

He nodded, called something in on his radio and turned toward the house, eyeing the closed front door and the empty porch. "I'll check things out."

"There was another officer here. He—"

"Yeah. We've got someone meeting him over at the bus depot. Wait here." He hurried into the house, and she was left standing in the yard.

She thought about calling Cassie and asking her to come. She didn't want to face things alone, but Cassie had enough on her plate. She didn't need to come running to the rescue every time Virginia had a little trouble.

Or a lot of it.

A second police cruiser pulled up behind the first. The passenger door opened, and Officer Forrester got out. He offered a quick wave before opening the back door and letting his dog out.

They made a striking team—both of them muscular and fit and a little ferocious looking. She'd met Officer Forrester at Cassie and Gavin's wedding. She hadn't paid all that much attention to him. She'd been trying to corral the kids, keep them from eating the cake or destroying flower arrangements. She'd heard a few of Cassie's other bridesmaids oohing and ahhing over the K-9 team members, but Virginia had no desire to ooh and ahh. She was way past the point of noticing men, and there was no way she planned to ever be involved in a relationship again.

"You doing okay?" Officer Forrester asked as he approached.

She nodded, because her throat still felt tight with fear, and she was afraid her voice would be shaky.

"I followed your guy to the bus depot. Samson lost the trail there. I think the perp might have gotten in a car, but it's possible he made it onto a bus. We'll check the security cameras in the area. See if we can figure out who he is and where he went."

"Good," she managed to say, her voice stronger than she expected it to be.

"You want to sit in your car while you wait?" he suggested, his gaze focused and intent, his eyes a bright crisp blue that reminded her of the summer sky.

"I'm fine."

"I'm sure you are, but you look pale, and Gavin asked me to keep an eye on you until he and Cassie get here."

"You called Gavin?"

"He's my supervisor," he responded as if that explained everything.

"Well, call him again," she said, because she didn't want her boss to come all the way from All Our Kids to help her. Not when there were two—she glanced at a tall blonde female officer getting out of the second cruiser—three police officers nearby. "Tell him that I'm fine and I don't need Cassie to come."

"How about you do that, Virginia?" he suggested. "I'm going in the house."

He was gone before she could respond, striding across the yard, Samson beside him.

She would have followed, but the female officer approached and began asking dozens of questions. Virginia answered the best she could, but her mind was on the house, the man she'd seen, the name he'd called her— Ginny. As if he'd said it a thousand times before.

No one called her Ginny. Not since Kevin had died.

No one in her new life, none of the new friends she'd made, the people she worked with, the kids she took care of knew that she'd ever gone by Ginny. For eight years, she'd been Virginia.

Whoever the guy in the house had been, he'd known her before. Or he'd known Kevin. She didn't like either thought. She didn't want to revisit the past. She didn't want to relive the weeks and months and years before she'd nearly died.

What she wanted to do was go back to her safe life working at All Our Kids. She wanted to forget about her inheritance, her past, all the nightmares that plagued her.

The front door of the house opened, and Officer Forrester appeared, the responding officer right behind him. They looked grim and unhappy, and she braced herself for bad news as she followed the female officer across the yard and up the porch stairs.

Virginia looked terrified.

John couldn't say he blamed her. Finding someone in a supposedly empty house would scare the bravest person. From what Gavin had told him, Virginia wasn't exactly that. As a matter of fact, Gavin had said Virginia tended to panic very quickly. Which was why he and Cassie were on their way to the house.

He wasn't going to call and tell them not to come, but Virginia seemed to be holding it together pretty well. No tears, no screams, no sobs. Just wide blue eyes, pale skin and soft hair falling across her cheeks.

"Did you find anything?" she asked, directing her question to the other officer.

Leonard Morris was a DC police officer. Well liked and respected, he knew just about every law enforcement officer in the district. "Nothing to write home about, ma'am," Officer Morris responded. "I'm going to dust for prints, but I thought you could come in, see if there's anything missing."

She hesitated for a heartbeat too long, her gaze jumping to the still-open front door, her skin going a shade paler. "I… Is that really necessary?"

Morris frowned. "If there's something missing, only you'll know it. So, yeah, I guess it is."

"I… Don't you want to dust for prints and look for evidence before I go in and contaminate the scene?"

"I think," John said, cutting in, taking her arm and urging her to the door, "it's been contaminated. You were already in there, remember?"

"I'm scared," she responded. "Not senile."

"Anyone would be scared in these circumstances."

"Maybe I didn't state my position strongly enough," she muttered as they stepped into the house. "I'm terrified, completely frozen with fear and unable to deal with this. Plus, up until today, I hadn't stepped foot in the house in eight years. I have no idea what Laurel had."

"You know what she had before. Maybe that will help. And you seem to be dealing just fine," he said, because she was. He'd seen people panic. He'd seen them so frozen with fear they couldn't act. Virginia didn't seem as if she was any of those things.

"For now. Let's see what happens if Kevin jumps out of a closet," she responded with a shaky laugh.

"Kevin?" Officer Morris asked.

Virginia frowned. "My husband. He died eight years ago."

"I guess he's not going to be jumping out of any closets, then," the female officer said, her gaze focused on the opulent staircase, the oil paintings that lined the wall leading upstairs. They screamed *money.* The whole place did.

"No. I guess he wouldn't, Officer...?"

"Glenda Winters. You want to tell me why you're worried about your dead husband jumping out of closets?" she asked.

John had worked with her before. She was a good police officer with a knack for getting the perp, but she was straightforward and matter-of-fact to a fault, her sharp interview tactics often getting her in trouble with her supervisor.

"I'm not," Virginia replied, walking into a huge living room, her gaze drifting across furniture, paintings and a grand piano that sat in an alcove jutting off from the main room. "It's just that the man who was in the house looked a lot like Kevin."

"They say everyone has a twin," Officer Morris commented.

"He called me Ginny. Just like Kevin used to," Virginia said, and for the first time since she'd come screaming through the bushes, John could actually see her shutting down and freezing up.

"Did Kevin have a brother?" he asked, and she shook her head, her eyes a little glassy, her skin pale as paper.

"No."

"How about cousins? Uncles? Extended family?" Officer Winters asked. "Because I have a cousin who looks so much like me, people think we're twins."

"If he does, I never met any of them."

"This was Laurel Johnson's place, right?" Officer Morris walked through the living room and into a dining area that could have seated twenty people comfortably.

"Yes. I'm her granddaughter-in-law."

Morris nodded. "She left you the property. Interesting, huh?"

Something seemed to pass between them, some unspoken words that John really wanted to hear, because there was an undercurrent in the house, a strange vibe that Virginia had brought inside with her. He wanted to know what it was, why it was there, what it had to do with the guy she'd seen in the house.

"I guess it is." Virginia took one last look around the living room. "As far as I can tell, nothing is missing," she said, then hurried into the dining room, the kitchen, up the back stairs and onto the second floor. With every step she seemed to sink deeper into herself, her eyes hollow and haunted, her expression blank.

Officer Morris whispered something in her ear, and she shook her head.

"I'm fine," she murmured, opening the first door and stepping into a nearly empty room. A cradle sat in the center of it, a few blankets piled inside. Pink. Blue. Yellow. There was a dresser, too. White and intricately carved, the legs swirling lion claws. No mementos, though. Not a picture, stuffed animal or toy.

"Everything looks okay in here," Virginia said, and tried to back out of the room.

Only John was standing behind her, and she backed into him.

He grabbed her shoulders, trying to keep her from toppling over. He felt narrow bones and taut muscles before she jerked away, skirted past him.

"Sorry."

"No need to apologize," he said, but she was already running to the next door to drag it open and dart inside.

THREE

Laurel had kept the nursery just the way it had been the day Kevin died. Being in it brought back memories Virginia had shoved so far back in her mind, she hadn't even known they were there—all the dreams about children and a family and creating something wonderful together, all the long conversations late at night when she and Kevin had shared their visions of the future. Only every word Kevin uttered had been designed to manipulate her, to make her believe that she could have all the things she longed for, so that he could have what he'd wanted—complete control. She'd believed him because she'd wanted to. She'd been a fool, and it had nearly cost her her life.

She wanted out of the house so desperately, she would have run downstairs and out the door if three police officers and a dog weren't watching her every move.

The dog, she thought, was preferable to the people. He, at least, looked sweet, his dark eyes following her as she moved through Laurel's room.

This was the same, too. Same flowered wallpaper that Virginia had helped her hang, same curtains that they'd picked out together in some posh bohemian shop in the heart of DC. Same antique headboard, same oversize rolltop desk that had been handed down from one generation to the other since before the revolutionary war.

It had always been closed before, the dark mahogany cover pulled down over the writing area and the dozens of tiny drawers and secret hiding places that Laurel had once shown her.

It was open now, and Virginia walked to it, ignoring the officers who walked into the room behind her. At least one of them knew her story. She wasn't sure how she felt about that. She'd refused to speak with reporters after the attack. It had taken a while, but eventually they'd lost interest and the story she'd lived through, the horrible nightmare that so many people had wanted the details of, had faded from the spotlight.

Eight years later, there were very few people who remembered. Those who did, didn't associate Virginia's face with the Johnson family tragedy. She'd never been in the limelight anyway. Kevin had preferred to stand there himself.

The older officer knew. He'd whispered a couple words that he'd probably thought would be comforting— *It's okay. He can't hurt you anymore.*

Only the words hadn't been comforting.

They'd just made her want to cry, because she was *that* woman. The one who'd met and married a monster. The one who'd almost been killed by the person who was supposed to love her more than he loved anyone else.

She yanked open one of the desk drawers, staring blindly at its contents.

Something nudged her leg, and she looked down; the huge German shepherd sat beside her, his tail thumping, his mouth in a facsimile of a smile.

She couldn't help herself. She smiled in return. "Are

you in a hurry, Samson?" she asked, and the dog cocked his head to the side, nudging her leg again.

Not a "hurry up" nudge, she didn't think. More of an "I'm here" nudge. Whatever it was, it made her feel a little more grounded, a little less in the past and a little more in the moment.

She rifled through the drawer. Laurel kept her spare keys there. House. Car. Attic. She took that one, because she was going to have to check up there. The entire space had been insulated and made into a walk-in storage area filled with centuries' worth of family heirlooms.

She opened another drawer. This one had stamps, envelopes, beautiful handmade pens.

It took ten minutes to go through every drawer, to open every secret compartment. She took out a beautiful mother's ring that Kevin had presented to Laurel years before he met Virginia. Laurel had worn it every day, and as far as Virginia knew, she'd never taken it off. Not when Kevin had been alive.

She set the ring on the desktop and took a strand of pearls from another secret compartment. The jewelry piled up. So did the old coins and the cash—nearly a thousand dollars' worth of that. Laurel had liked to have cash on hand. Just in case.

"That's a lot of money, right there," Officer Forrester said quietly. "I'd think if the guy were here to steal, he'd have left the desk empty."

"Maybe he didn't have time to go through it." She rolled the desktop down, leaving the jewelry and money right where it was. The words felt hollow, her heart beating a hard harsh rhythm. She wanted to believe the guy had been there looking for easy cash but the sick feeling of dread in her stomach was telling her otherwise.

"That's a possibility," Officer Winters said, her voice

sharp. "It's also possible he found other valuables and took off with them. You said you hadn't been here in a while. He could have left with thousands of dollars' worth of stolen property."

I don't really care if he did. I never wanted any of this. I still don't, she wanted to say, but she didn't, because there wasn't a person she knew who wouldn't have celebrated the windfall Virginia had received. The few friends she'd told had given her dozens of ideas for what she could do with the money, the house, the antiques. Most of the ideas involved quitting her job, going on trips to Europe and Asia, traveling the country, finding Mr. Right.

She hadn't told anyone but Cassie that she didn't want the inheritance. Even Cassie didn't know the entire reason why.

Or maybe she did.

She was her boss, after all. There'd been a background check when Virginia had applied for the job. If the information about Kevin had come up, Cassie had kept it to herself. She'd never questioned Virginia, never brought up the life Virginia had lived before taking the job at All Our Kids.

That was the way Virginia wanted it.

No reminders of the past. No questions about why and how she'd ended up married to a monster. No sympathetic looks and whispered comments. She didn't want to be that woman, that wife, that abused spouse.

She just wanted to be the person she'd been before she'd fallen for Kevin.

It had taken years to realize that wasn't possible. By that time, keeping quiet about what she'd been through had become a habit. One she had no intention of breaking.

She walked to an old oil painting that hung between

two bay windows and pulled it from the wall, revealing the built-in safe that Laurel had shown her a year after she'd moved into the house, a day after Kevin had shoved her for the first time.

Maybe Laurel had thought seeing all the beautiful jewels that would be hers one day would keep Virginia from going to the police.

It hadn't.

Love had.

She hadn't wanted Kevin to be arrested. She hadn't wanted to ruin his reputation and his career. She'd believed his tearful apology, and she'd believed to the depth of her soul that he would change. She'd been wrong, of course. Sometimes, she thought that she'd always known it. Even then. Even the first time.

She knew the lock combination by heart, and she opened the safe. It was stuffed full of all the wonderful things that Laurel had collected over the years. Her husband had been generous. He'd showered her with expensive gifts.

She pulled out a velvet bag and poured six beautiful sapphire rings into her palm. Seeing them made her want to puke, because they were the first things Laurel had pulled out the day she'd opened the safe and shown Virginia everything she would inherit one day.

She gagged, tossing the rings into the safe and running to the en suite bathroom. She heard someone call her name, but she wasn't in the mood for listening. She slammed the door, turned the lock, sat on the cold tile floor and dropped her head to her knees.

If she'd had one tear left for all the lies she'd been told and believed, if she'd had one bit of grief for what she'd longed for and lost, she'd have cried.

She didn't, so she just sat where she was, the soft mur-

mur of voices drifting through the door, while she prayed that she could do what she knew she had to—face the past and move on with her life. It was the only way she'd ever find the sweet spot, the lovely place where she was exactly where God wanted her to be, doing exactly what He wanted her doing.

No more floundering around waiting for other people to call the shots. No more watching as life passed by. She wanted to engage in the process of living again. She wanted to do more than be a housemother to kids. She wanted to mentor them. She wanted to be an example to them. She wanted to be able to tell her story without embarrassment or shame, and she wanted other people to benefit from it.

That was what she thought about late at night when she couldn't sleep and all she had were her prayers and the still, soft voice that told her she was wasting time being afraid, wasting her life worrying about making the wrong choices.

She needed to change that.

The problem was, she wasn't sure how.

Someone knocked on the door, and she pushed to her feet, her bones aching, her muscles tight. She felt a thousand years old, but she managed to walk to the door and open it.

Officer Forrester was there, Samson beside him. The other two officers were gone.

"I'm sorry," she said. "I just—"

"You don't have to explain." He took her elbow, leading her back into the room.

"I feel like I do, Officer—"

"John. I'm not on duty." He smiled, and his face softened, all the hard lines and angles easing into something pleasant and approachable.

"You chased down the guy who was in my house."

"Tried to, but only because I was in the right place at the right time."

"Or the wrong place at the wrong time."

He chuckled. "I guess that depends on how you look at it. I see it as a good thing. But, then, I love what I do, and I'm always happy to step in and help when I can."

"That's...unusual."

"You seem awfully young to be so jaded, Virginia."

"I'm not young."

"Sure you are." He opened Laurel's closet, whistling softly. "Wow. This lady had some clothes."

"She did." She moved in beside him, eyeing the contents of the walk-in closet. Dresses. Shoes. Belts. Handbags. "I guess if the guy didn't take a bunch of cash and jewelry, he probably didn't take any of her clothes."

"Do you think that was what he was here for?" he asked. "Money?"

"That's what the police think he was here for."

"I'm not asking about the police. I'm asking about you. Do you think he was here for money or valuables?"

It was a simple question.

At least in John's mind it was.

Virginia didn't seem able to answer it.

She stared at him, her face pale, her eyes deeply shadowed.

"Okay. You're not going to answer that," he said. "So, how about you tell me why it's been so many years since you've been in the house?"

She shook her head. "It's not important."

"If it weren't, you'd be willing to tell me about it."

"Maybe I should have said that it's important to me but has no bearing on what happened today."

"You can't know that."

"The police seem to think—"

"I think that I already said that I'm not interested in what the police are saying. You know this house, you knew your grandmother-in-law. You knew your husband, and every time you mention that the guy who was here looked like Kevin, I can almost see the wheels turning behind your eyes. You're thinking something. I'd like to know what it is."

"I'm thinking that I could have been wrong about what I saw. Maybe the guy didn't look as much like Kevin as I'd thought." She closed the closet door and walked to a fireplace that took up most of one wall. There were a few photos on the mantel. He hadn't looked closely, but he thought they must be of Virginia's family. She lifted one, smiling a little as she looked at the image of a young man and woman in wedding finery. Probably taken in the fifties, it was a little faded, the framed glass covered with a layer of dust. She swiped dust from the glass, set it back down, and John waited, because he thought there was more she wanted to say.

Finally, she turned to face him again. "My husband wasn't the easiest man to live with. I have a lot of bad memories. I really don't like talking about them."

That explained a lot, but it didn't explain who had been in her house or why he'd been there.

"I'm sorry. I know that's got to be tough to live with," he said.

"Some days, it's harder than others." She looked around the room, and he thought she might be fighting tears. She didn't cry, though, just cleared her throat, and smoothed her hair. "I know you're trying to help, and I appreciate it, but Officer Morris already knows everything there is to know. If he's worried that this is connected to…my past. He'll let me know."

That should have been enough to send John on his

way. After all, this wasn't his case. Morris and Winters were calling the shots. He was just a witness who happened to be a police officer, but he didn't want to leave. Not when Virginia still looked so shaken.

"Morris is a great police officer, and he'll handle things well, but I'm your neighbor. If something happens, I'm the closest thing to help you've got. Keep that in mind, okay?"

"I will." She hesitated, her fingers trailing over another photo. "The thing is, something did happen. I almost died eight years ago. Right outside the front door of this place. Not even the neighbors were able to help. That's why I haven't been back. That's why I don't like talking about it. That's why I don't want to believe the guy I saw today has anything to do with Kevin."

The words were stated without emotion, but he read a boatload of feelings in her face. Fear, sadness, anxiety. Shame. That was the big one, and he'd seen it one too many times—a woman who'd done nothing wrong, feeling shame for what she'd been through.

"Your husband?" he asked, and she nodded, lifting another photo from the mantel. She was in it, white flowers in her hair, wearing a simple white dress that fell to her feet.

"This is my wedding photo. I guess Laurel cut Kevin out of it. We were married in Maui. A beautiful beach wedding with five hundred guests."

"Wow."

"I know. It was excessive. We footed the bill. I would have preferred to use the money to finish my doctorate, but Kevin…" She shook her head. "It was a long time ago. It doesn't matter."

"It matters to you," he responded.

"It shouldn't." She replaced the picture she was still

holding. "I should check the other rooms, see if anything has been disturbed."

She walked into the hall, and he didn't stop her.

He wanted to take a closer look at the photos on the mantel. The one of Virginia didn't look as if it had been cut. He opened the back of the frame and carefully lifted the photo out.

It had been folded.

He smoothed it out, eyeing the smiling dark-haired man who stood to Virginia's right. Not touching her. Which seemed odd. It was a wedding photo, after all. The guy had a shot glass in one hand, a bottle of bourbon in the other. He looked drunk, his eyes heavy-lidded, his grin sloppy.

He replaced the photo and looked at the others. Nothing stood out to him. They were all of the 1950s couple— marriage, new house, baby dressed in blue.

Kevin's father? If so, there were no other pictures of him. No toddler pictures. No school photos. No wedding picture. That made John curious. There was a story there, and he had a feeling that it was somehow related to the man who'd been in the house.

It wasn't his case, and it wasn't any of his business, but he planned to mention it to Morris. See if he knew more about the Johnson family than Virginia did.

Or more than she was willing to reveal.

That was going to have to change. There was no way she could be allowed to keep her secrets. She'd have to open up, say everything she knew, everything she suspected, because John had a bad feeling that the guy who'd been in her house had been after a lot more than a few bucks. He'd been after Virginia, and if she wasn't careful, he just might get what he wanted.

FOUR

The police thought the intruder had entered through the kitchen. The lock hadn't been tampered with, but there were a couple of muddy footprints on the back deck and a pair of old size ten boots sitting under the swing.

They weren't Kevin's. He'd always worn Italian leather. Dress shoes shined to a high sheen paired with suits he spent a small fortune on. Even if he'd worn boots, Virginia didn't think they'd have been sitting out on the back deck years after his death.

They belonged to someone. So did the clothes she'd found in the closet in the bedroom she hadn't wanted to enter. The bedroom she and Kevin had shared. She'd gone in anyway, found faded jeans and threadbare T-shirts hanging in a closet that had once been filled with Kevin's clothes. Kevin had never worn jeans, had rarely worn T-shirts. No, the clothes had belonged to someone else. Officer Morris had taken them as evidence. Virginia wasn't sure what kind of evidence he could get from them. Hair? DNA? She hadn't asked. She'd been too busy trying not to panic.

Now she was alone, the officers gone, the house silent. She paced the living room, cold to the bone. She'd turned the heat on high, turned every light in the house on. She'd made tea and drunk two cups, but she couldn't get warm.

Someone had been in the house.

Someone who'd looked like Kevin, who'd called her Ginny, who'd mocked her with words that had made her blood run like ice through her veins.

A friend of Kevin's?

If so, he wasn't someone she'd ever met.

Whoever he was, he'd been in the house for a while. The clothes, the boots. The police had agreed that the guy had spent some time there.

That meant he'd had plenty of time to take whatever he might have wanted, but the house seemed untouched, hundreds of valuable things left behind.

She rubbed her arms, trying to chase away the chill. It didn't work. It was the house, the memories. She'd thought about going to a hotel, but she had to do this, and she had to do it alone. Cassie had offered to stay the night, babysit her like she babysat the children at All Our Kids. Virginia had refused her offer.

At the time, the sun had still been up.

Now it had set, the last rays tingeing the sky with gold and pink. If she just looked at that, stared out the window and watched the sky go black, she might be okay.

She would be okay.

Because there was nothing to be afraid of. Gavin had changed the lock on the back and front doors; he'd checked the locks on all the windows. The house was secure. That should have made her feel better. It didn't.

She grabbed her overnight bag and walked up the stairs, the wood creaking beneath her feet. She knew the sounds the treads made. She knew the groan of the landing, the soft hiss of the furnace. She knew the house with all its quirks, but she still felt exposed and afraid, nervous in a way she hadn't been in years.

She thought about calling Cassie, just to hear someone else's voice, but if she did that, Cassie would come running to the rescue.

That wasn't what Virginia wanted.

What she wanted was peace. The hard-won kind that came from conquering the beasts that had been controlling her for too long.

Outside, the neighborhood quieted as people settled in for an evening at home. That was the kind of place this was—weekend parties and weeknight quiet. Older, well-established families doing what they'd done for generations—living well and nicely.

Only things weren't always nice there.

She'd learned that the hard way.

She grabbed a blanket from the linen closet. There was no way she was sleeping in any of the bedrooms. She'd sleep on the couch with her cell phone clutched in her hand. Just in case.

She *would* sleep, though.

She'd promised herself that.

She wouldn't spend the night pacing and jumping at shadows.

Only it had been years since she'd lived alone, years since she'd not had noise to fill the silences. The sounds of children whispering and giggling, the soft pad of feet on the floor, those were part of her life. Without them all she could hear were her own thoughts.

She settled onto the couch, pulling the blanket around her shoulders. It smelled of dust and loneliness. She tried not to think about Laurel, spending the last years of her life alone. No kids to visit her. No husband. No grandchildren. Just Laurel living in this mausoleum of a house, shuffling from room to room, dusting and cleaning compulsively the way she had when Virginia lived there.

She couldn't sleep with that thought or with the musty blanket wrapped around her shoulders. She shoved it off, lay on her side, staring out the front window, wishing the night away.

She must have drifted off.

She woke to the sound of rain tapping against the roof and the subtle scent of cigarette smoke drifting in the air.

Cigarette smoke?

Her pulse jumped, and she inhaled deeply, catching the scent again. Just a tinge of something acrid and a little sharp lingering.

Was it coming from outside?

In the house?

She crept to the doorway that led into the hall and peered into the foyer. The front door was closed. Just the way she'd left it, but the scent of smoke was thicker there, and she glanced up the stairs, terrified that she'd see *him* again.

She saw nothing. Not him. Not the light that should have been shining from the landing.

The upstairs hallway was dark as pitch, and she was sure she saw something moving in the blackness. The shadow of a man? The swirl of smoke?

She didn't care. She wanted out.

She lunged for the door, scrambling with the lock and racing onto the porch. Her car was in the driveway, but she hadn't brought her keys, and the phone that she'd been clutching to her chest when she fell asleep? Gone.

She must have dropped it.

She should have thought to look for it before she went searching the house for a cigarette-smoking intruder.

She ran down the porch stairs, her bare feet slapping against wet wood. She made it halfway across the yard before she saw the man standing on the sidewalk. She skidded to a stop, her heart beating frantically, as she watched the butt of his cigarette arch through the darkness.

"Everything okay?" he asked, his face illuminated by the streetlights, his little dog sniffing around at his feet.

"I..." What could she say? That she'd smelled his cigarette and thought someone was in the house? She doubted he'd want to know all the details of that. "Fine..."

"Probably you should put some shoes on. This isn't just rain. It's ice—and your feet are going to freeze."

Her feet were already freezing, but she didn't mention that. She was too relieved to have found the smoker outside her house to be worried about her feet. She thanked him and walked back to the house. The door was open as she approached, just the way she'd left it.

She'd nearly reached it when it swung closed.

She grabbed the door handle, trying to push it open again.

It was locked.

She hadn't paid much attention when Gavin had been installing it. Was it the kind of knob that locked automatically?

One way or another, she was locked outside.

Which, she thought, might be for the best.

The door might have closed on its own. There was a slight breeze. It was also possible she'd imagined the shadow in the upstairs hallway. She'd imagined plenty of other things before—faces staring out of the dark corners of rooms she knew were empty, shadowy figures standing at the foot of her bed when she was just waking from nightmares. None of those things had ever turned out to be real, but right at that moment, she was certain someone was in the house, and she was just as certain that if she entered it, she might not come out alive.

She didn't have her phone, didn't know any of the neighbors. She'd given Gavin and Cassie the spare keys to the house, but she had no way of contacting either of them. She did know John Forrester, though, and he'd told her to call if she had any trouble. She didn't know what time it was. She didn't care. She jogged around the side of the house and headed toward his garage apartment.

Samson growled, the sound a soft warning that pulled John from sleep. He sat up, scanning the dark room for signs of trouble. The living room was empty, the TV still on whatever station John had been watching when he'd fallen asleep on the couch.

"What is it, boy?" he asked, keeping the light off as he walked to the window where the dog was standing.

The dog growled again, nudging at the glass, his gaze fixed on some point beyond the yard.

Virginia's house?

John leaned closer, peering out into the blackness. Ice fell from the inky sky, glittering on the trees and grass, tapping against the garage roof. Not a good night to be out, but he thought he saw a shadow moving near the shrubs. As he watched, it darted through the thick foliage, sprinted into the open.

Medium height. Slim.

Virginia?

Samson stopped growling, gave a soft whine that meant he recognized the person running toward the garage.

Virginia, for sure, and it looked as if she was in trouble.

He ran to the door, yanked it open. He was halfway down the stairs when Virginia appeared. She barreled toward him, wet hair hanging in her face, head down as she focused on keeping her footing on the slippery stairs.

"Everything okay?" he asked.

It was obvious everything wasn't.

She had bare feet, no coat, skin so pale it nearly glowed in the darkness.

"I'm running through an ice storm in bare feet," she responded. "Things are not okay."

"What's going on?" he asked, grabbing her hand, urging her up the last few stairs and into the apartment.

"I locked myself out of the house." Her teeth chattered, and he grabbed the throw from the back of the couch and dropped it around her shoulders.

"Should I ask why you were outside in the middle of the night?"

"I smelled cigarette smoke and thought it was coming from inside the house."

He didn't like the sound of that.

The police hadn't found cigarette butts on the property, but that didn't mean the guy who'd been there wasn't a smoker. "I'll go check things out," he said, grabbing Samson's work lead and calling the dog.

"Don't go rushing over there yet, John. I'm not done with my story."

"The ending isn't as exciting as the beginning?" he asked, grabbing a towel from the linen closet and handing it to her.

"I'm not sure." She wiped moisture from her face and hair, then tucked a few strands of hair behind her ear. "The cigarette smoke was coming from outside. Some guy walking his dog. When I went to go back in, the door closed."

"The wind?" he suggested, and she shrugged.

"That would be a logical explanation."

"But?" he prodded, because he thought there was

more to the story, and he wasn't sure why she was holding back.

"I'm going to be honest with you," she said with a sigh. "I was diagnosed with PTSD a few years ago. I went to counseling, worked through a lot of issues, but I still have nightmares. I still wake up in the middle of the night and think someone is standing in my room or hiding in the shadows. Sometimes I think there's danger when there isn't."

This was part of what she hadn't told him earlier. She'd hinted at it, said she'd nearly died, but she hadn't given details. He'd done a little digging and asked a few questions. Morris hadn't been eager to give details, but there'd been a few newspaper articles written about it. Local Attorney Shoots Wife and Self in Apparent Murder-Suicide Attempt.

Lots of speculation as to why it had happened, but there'd been no interviews with Virginia or her grandmother-in-law, so no one knew for sure how a seemingly rational high-level attorney could snap.

Personally, John didn't think he'd snapped. He thought the guy had been out of control from the get-go, that he'd just been hiding it from the world.

"The worst mistake you can make—" he began, taking the towel from her hand and using it to wipe moisture from the back of her hair. The strands were long and thick and curling from the rain, and he could see hints of gold and red mixed with light brown "—is hesitating to ask for help because you doubt your ability to distinguish real danger from imagined danger."

"I think I've proven—"

"You've proven that you're strong and smart," he said, cutting her off, because thinking about what she'd been through, the way she'd probably spent her entire marriage—in fear and self-doubt and even guilt—made him want to go back in time, meet her jerk of a husband and teach him a lesson about how women should be treated. "You might jump at shadows, but you're not calling for the cavalry every time it happens."

"I guess that's true," she conceded with a half smile. She had a little color in her cheeks, a little less hollowness in her eyes.

"So, tell me what happened with the door. You don't think it was the wind." Not a question, but she shook her head.

"I turned all the lights on in the house."

He'd noticed that, but he didn't say as much, just let her continue speaking.

"Then I went downstairs, lay down on the couch and fell asleep. When I woke, the lights upstairs were off."

"Power outage, maybe?"

"The other lights were still on."

"Did you check the circuit breaker? Maybe you blew a fuse. It happens in old houses."

"I might have checked, if I'd been able to get back in the house. The door locked when it closed. I couldn't remember if Gavin installed a lock that does that, but..." She shuddered and pulled the blanket a little tighter around her shoulders.

"I don't think he did." And that worried John. There'd been evidence that the guy who'd been in Virginia's house had stayed there for a while—clothes in the closet, an unmade bed. It could be that he'd returned, found a way in, gone back to whatever he was doing before Virginia had arrived. "Tell you what. Stay here. Samson and I will go check things out."

"I gave the spare key to Gavin and Cassie, and the doors are all locked."

"I'll call Gavin and ask him to meet me at your place.

I'll call Officer Morris, too. He should know what's going on." He attached Samson's lead, and every muscle in the dog's body tensed with excitement.

Samson loved his job, and John loved working with him. He was one of the smartest, most eager animals John had ever trained.

"Heel," he commanded as he stepped outside. "Lock the door, Virginia. I'll be back as soon as I can."

FIVE

John called Gavin on the way down the stairs and asked him to call Officer Morris. He didn't want to make the call himself. He knew what the DC officer would say—stay clear of the scene. Let the local police handle things.

Wasn't going to happen.

If someone was in the house, John planned to find him. Virginia had been through enough. He wasn't going to stand by and watch her be tormented. So far, that was what seemed to be happening. No overt threats of danger, no physical attacks, the guy seemed more interested in terrifying her than in hurting her.

That could change, though, and John wasn't willing to wait for it to happen.

The upstairs lights were on when John arrived at the house. He could see them gleaming through the windows. That didn't mean they hadn't been off when Virginia woke. He kept that in mind as he eased around the building, Samson sniffing the air, his ears alert, his tail high. Focused, but not cautious. So far, the dog didn't sense any danger.

They moved around to the front of the house, and Samson headed straight across the yard, sniffing at a soggy cigarette butt that lay on the sidewalk. It seemed odd that Virginia had been able to smell the smoke.

He left the butt where it was and walked to the porch, Samson on-heel. The dog nosed the floorboards, sniffed the air, growled.

"Find," John commanded, and the dog raced off the porch and around the side of the house, sniffing the ground, then the air. He nosed a bush that butted up against the edge of the house, alerting there before he ran to a window that was cracked open. No way had Virginia left it that way. Someone who'd been through what she had didn't leave windows open and doors unlocked.

Samson scratched at the window, barking twice. He smelled his quarry, and he wanted to get into the house and follow the scent to the prize.

"Hold," John said, and the dog subsided, sitting on his haunches, his eyes still trained on the window.

John eased it open. The screen had been cut, and that made his blood run cold. Virginia's instincts had been spot-on. Someone had been in the house with her.

A loud bang broke the silence, and Samson jumped up, barking frantically, pulling at the lead. John let him have his lead following him to the back of the house. A dark shadow sprinted across the yard. Tall. Thin. Fair skin.

"Freeze!" he called, but the guy kept going.

"Stop or I'll release my dog," he shouted the warning, and the guy hesitated, turning a little in their direction, something flashing in his hand.

A gun!

John dove for cover, landing on his stomach as the first bullet slammed into the upper story of the house. He pulled his weapon, but the perp had already darted behind the neighbor's house. No way was John taking a blind shot. It was too dangerous for the neighbors, for anyone who happened to wander outside to see what all the commotion was about.

He unhooked Samson's lead, releasing the dog, allowing him to do what he did best.

Samson moved across the yard, his muscular body eating up the ground. No hesitation. No slowing down. He had unerring accuracy when it came to finding suspects, and the guy they were seeking was close. No amount of running would get him out of range, because Samson would never give up the hunt.

John sprinted across the yard, knowing Samson would alert when he had the perp cornered. Ice crackled under his feet as he rounded the neighbor's house, racing into the front yard. Samson was just ahead, bounding across the street and into a small park lined with trees. The perp had plenty of cover there, plenty of places to hide and take aim.

"Release," he called, and Samson slowed, stopped, sending John a look that said *why are you ending the game?*

"Let's be careful, pal," John said, hooking the lead back on. "The guy has a gun." And he'd already discharged it.

They moved through the trees and farther into the park, Samson's muscles taut as he searched for the scent. When he found it, he barked once and took off running. The darkness pressed in on all sides. No light from the street here. Just the ice falling from the sky and the muted sound of cars driving through the neighborhood.

Behind them, branches snapped and feet pounded on the ground. A dog barked, and John knew that backup had arrived. He glanced over his shoulder, saw Dylan Ralsey and his dog Tico heading toward him.

"Gavin called. I was closer than he was, and he thought

you could use some backup," Dylan said as he scanned the darkness. "His ETA is ten minutes."

"Thanks," John replied. He didn't stop. They didn't have time to discuss what had happened, go over the details, come up with a plan.

"Tico was bored anyway. It's been a slow night." Dylan moved in beside him, flanking his right, Tico on his lead a little ahead.

The park opened out into another quiet street. Both dogs stopped at the curb, nosed the ground, whined.

"He had a car," John said, disgusted with himself for letting the guy escape.

"Wonder if any of the neighbors have security cameras? Seems like that kind of neighborhood, don't you think?" Dylan asked.

It did.

The houses were large, well maintained and expensive. Lights shone from porches and highlighted security signs posted in several yards.

"That would almost be too easy, wouldn't it? Look at some security footage, get a license plate number, find our guy?" he murmured more to himself than to Dylan.

"We can't assume the guy was driving his own car, but if we could get a tag number on whatever he was driving?" Dylan smiled through the darkness. "We'll have something to go on."

"Did Gavin mention whether or not Morris sent the clothes we found this afternoon to the evidence lab?"

"Not to me, but if they were sent, it might be weeks before you hear anything. If they can find some DNA, there might be a match in the system."

"Finding one will take even more time that Virginia might not have. The perp is bold. He entered the house while she was sleeping, and he had a gun."

"Did he fire it?"

"Hit the side of the house. The bullet should be lodged in the siding."

"We might get some ballistic evidence from it."

"You mean Morris might," John said. "He's the local PD who's handling the case."

"I know who he is. Gavin told me to steer clear of the guy."

"Guess Morris isn't all that happy with my involvement."

"From what Gavin said, he's on his way, and he's not happy. Said you needed to stop stepping on his toes or things could get ugly."

"Should I sit back and watch a woman be terrorized?" John asked, allowing Samson to nose the ground, follow whatever scent he could to the east.

"As a fellow member of the Capitol K-9 Unit, I'm going to have to say yes. Because that's the official protocol."

"What would you say as my friend?"

"You know what I'd say, John. Do what you have to do to keep Virginia safe."

"I guess you know which way I'm going to go," John responded, because he couldn't sit back and watch crimes be committed, he couldn't back off and wait for help to arrive when he could be the one doing the helping. It was the way he'd been raised. His father, grandfather, brother, had all been police officers. They'd all given their lives for their jobs, sacrificing everything to see justice done.

"I guess I do."

Samson stopped at a crossroad, circled twice, then sat on his haunches. He'd lost the trail. Not surprising. He was trained in apprehension and guard duty. Scent trail wasn't his forte, though he'd done some training in that, as well.

"Good try, champ," John said, scratching the dog behind the ears and offering the praise he deserved.

"The perp is heading toward downtown," Dylan said, his gaze focused on the road that led out of the community. "If we had a description of the vehicle, I could call it in, get some officers looking for it."

"Anyone who confronts the guy is going to have to be careful. He isn't afraid to use his weapon."

Dylan scowled. "That's not news that fills me with warm fuzzy feelings."

"I wasn't too thrilled, either."

"You'd be even less thrilled if you were lying in a hospital bed."

"True, but I don't think the guy was aiming for me. I think he was just trying to get me to back off."

"So, he's playing games?"

That was the feeling John had, so he nodded. "That's the impression that I'm getting."

He'd dealt with plenty of criminals. He'd had a few occasions when he'd been certain he was looking evil in the face. He was trained to understand the way felons would respond in a variety of situations, and he had a reputation for being good at staying a step ahead of the bad guys.

Sometimes, though, crimes weren't about what could be gained. They weren't about revenge or jealousy or passion. Sometimes they were a fantasy being played out, a game whose rules only the perpetrator knew.

He thought this was one of those times.

If he was right, the perp's next move couldn't be predicted. How he'd act or react couldn't be ascertained.

The best thing they could do was find him quickly

and get him off the street; because until he was locked away, Virginia wouldn't be safe.

One. Two. Three. Four. Five.

Virginia mentally counted houses with Christmas lights while she waited for Officer Morris to finish typing whatever it was he was typing into his tablet.

Six. Seven. Eight.

She hadn't learned much about what had happened at Laurel's place, but she could say for sure that John had a good view of the neighborhood from his kitchen window—houses, streets, the city beyond, all of it covered with a layer of ice that sparkled with reflected light.

It would be a mess for the commute in the morning, but right then, it was lovely. So were the Christmas lights hung from eaves and wound around columns and pillars. Several trees were decorated for the holiday. Most of them with soft blue or white lights. Very elegant and lovely, but that was the type of community they were in.

Nine. Ten. Eleven.

Officer Morris continued to type, and Virginia continued to count, because it was easier to do that than think about the gunshot she'd heard. No one had been injured. That's what Officer Morris had told her, but she hadn't heard from John, and she was worried.

Because worrying was something she excelled at. Apparently so was counting.

Dealing with emergencies? Not so much.

She almost hadn't opened the door when Officer Morris knocked. She'd been too afraid of who might be on the other side.

"Okay," Officer Morris said. "The report is filled out. We're good to go. How about we walk you back to your place, take a look around? Aside from a cut screen and busted window lock, I didn't see anything that looked out of place, but it would be best for you to take a look before I leave."

Her place.

Right.

She kept thinking of it as Laurel's or Kevin's or the Johnsons', but it belonged to her, and she had to go home to it. At least for the next few days.

"I should probably wait for John to return."

"He'll meet us at the house. I need to speak with him." There was no question in Officer Morris's voice. He had a plan, and he expected that everyone was going to follow it.

She didn't mind that. She didn't mind *him*. He seemed like a good guy, a nice cop. The fact that he knew what had happened to her…that was a little awkward, but he wasn't treating her with kid gloves, and she appreciated that.

She still didn't want to go back to the house.

Not after *he'd* been in it again. The guy who looked like Kevin. She hadn't seen him, but she was certain that was who it had been. Two different intruders in less than twenty-four hours seemed like too much of a stretch.

Yeah. It had been him. He'd broken the lock, cut the screen, entered the house. All while she'd been sleeping.

She shuddered, pulling the blanket John had given her closer.

Officer Morris's expression softened, and he touched her shoulder. "It's going to be fine, Virginia. He's gone. I promise you that."

She wasn't sure who he was talking about. The guy who looked like Kevin? Kevin?

Either way, he meant well, the words soothing and kind.

"Right. I know." She plastered a smile on her face. One that felt brittle and hard.

"I've been doing a little research," he said. Maybe he was hoping to distract her from the panic that was building. "Laurel Johnson was involved in a lot of charitable organizations."

"Yes," she responded, her mouth so dry it was all she could manage.

"One of them was the state prison ministry. She used to go there twice a week."

"I didn't know that."

"I doubt anyone did. She spent some time with one of the prisoners, helped him get his college degree. Name was Luke Miller. Ever heard of him?"

"No."

"He was released two months ago."

She wasn't sure what he was saying, what he was trying to get at. She was still thinking about going back to the house, walking into the place that had brought every nightmare she'd ever lived through.

"You look a little shaky. How about some water before we head over?" he suggested.

She nodded, mute with fear.

He walked into the kitchen, found a cup and filled it. "It really is going to be okay," he said, holding out the cup.

She took a step forward, felt the earth shake, the entire world rumble. For a moment, she thought she'd lost it, that it had finally happened, panic making her completely lose touch with reality. She was on the floor, staring up at the ceiling, smoke billowing all around her.

Officer Morris shouted something, and she rolled to her side, saw him lying under the partially caved-in wall, ice falling on his dark hair.

"Get out of here!" he shouted.

She struggled to her knees, her feet, grabbed the wood that was pinning him.

"Go!" he said again, and she shook her head, tugged harder, praying that somehow her strength would be enough to free him.

SIX

Smoke billowed up into the sky, flames licking the side of the garage as John raced toward his apartment. He'd expected trouble, but he hadn't expected this. He should have. He should have been prepared for anything.

Too late now.

The building was in flames, the interior exposed on the lower and upper levels.

A bomb?

That was what it looked like.

If there were more, they'd all be killed, but he wasn't going to wait for the fire department to show, couldn't wait for the bomb squad to be called in. Virginia and Officer Morris had been in the apartment. If they still were, they were in trouble.

"Hold!" he commanded, and Samson stopped short, his soft whimpers following John as he raced up the stairs that had been left untouched by the explosion.

The front door was closed. No time for a key, he kicked it in, smoke billowing out as it opened.

"Be careful!" Dylan shouted as he raced up the stairs behind him. "This place could crumble any minute."

That was John's fear. Getting in and out as quickly as possible was his plan.

Only God knew if that would happen, and John had to trust that His plan was best, that He'd see him through this like He had so many other things.

He pulled his shirt up over his mouth and nose, then headed into what had once been his living room. Part of the ceiling and wall had caved in, icy rain the only thing keeping the fire from taking over. Smoke billowed up through the floor and in through the collapsed wall. In seconds, the place would be pitch-black.

He scanned the room.

Virginia stood in the kitchen, tugging at lumber that had fallen, her frantic cries for help barely carrying above the roaring of the fire below.

He moved toward her and saw Officer Morris as he reached her side. His legs pinned by a heavy beam, his eyes open and filled with fury, he gestured toward Virginia.

"Get her out of here!" Morris shouted.

"I think we can free you," he responded, refusing to give in to panic, to let himself imagine the floor giving way.

Dylan moved in beside him. "On three," he said. "One. Two."

"Three." And the beam was up, Morris rolling out from beneath it.

Morris managed to get to his feet, but stumbled to his knees.

"My legs are busted," he growled, pushing to his feet again. Black smoke made it nearly impossible to see the extent of the damage, but there was no pain in his voice. No concern.

He was in shock.

Had to be.

They'd deal with it when they got out.

"When I catch the guy who did this," Morris muttered, "I'm going to make sure he goes away for the rest of his life."

An idle threat if they didn't get out.

"I'll get him," Dylan said, nothing but a shadow in the darkness. "You get Virginia."

No more words after that. No air for it. Just a sense of where the door should be, the direction they had to go to survive.

John grabbed Virginia's hand, leading the way through the thickening smoke.

He felt dizzy…knew how close they all were to losing consciousness. If he was heading in the wrong direction, if he'd gotten disoriented, they'd die.

He felt the front door before he saw it, the cold air billowing in and carrying bits of freezing rain with it.

He gave Virginia a gentle shove out the door.

"Get down the stairs," he rasped. "Stay close to Samson."

Then he turned, heading back into the darkness.

Dylan was there somewhere, struggling to carry Morris out.

John could hear Virginia calling his name, but he didn't turn back.

All of them or none of them.

That was the way it was going to be.

She couldn't leave them.

Wouldn't.

Virginia stood in the threshold of the door, smoke choking off her words as she shouted for the three men. She had no light to flash into the darkness, but she could scream until she had no voice left.

Behind her, sirens screeched and a dog howled.

Samson?

She didn't have time to comfort him. The building seemed to shake on its foundation, the fire eating away at the support beams.

"Over here!" she screamed. "This way!"

She thought she heard a voice, thought she saw something dark moving through the smoke.

Please, God, she pleaded silently as she shouted again.

Then they were there, just in front of her.

She reached in, dragging someone out by his shirt.

A Capitol K-9 officer. Morris plastered to his side, barely moving. Dylan? She thought that was the officer's name, but she didn't have time to ask, didn't have time to care.

"Down the stairs!" he shouted.

"John—"

"Here." John appeared in the doorway. "Now go! This place is going down."

She ran, stumbled down the last few steps and fell to her knees on wet grass.

And then John had her by the arm, dragging her up again.

"Keep going!" he shouted.

She didn't have time to wonder why; they were racing across the grass, the other K-9 officer right beside them, Morris in a fireman's hold over his shoulder.

Behind them, something popped. She heard a whoosh, felt a hot wind blow against her back. She stumbled, but John's arm was around her, and she kept going.

Just ahead, a fire crew raced toward them, shouting words Virginia couldn't hear.

Someone pulled her from John, slapped an oxygen mask over her face. She wanted to say that she was fine, that they needed to take care of the men, but darkness was closing in. Not the night, the smoke, the icy storm—just the blackness. She felt it coming for her, and then she felt nothing at all.

If there was one thing John hated, it was hospitals.

He'd watched his father breathe his last in one, said goodbye to his grandfather in one, been called to one after his brother was fatally shot.

Yeah. Hospitals weren't his thing.

He strode to a sink in the tiny triage room they'd rolled him into, and scrubbed soot from his face and hands. The doctor had already been in once, listened to his lungs, ordered an X-ray. Everything had checked out. Now, he was waiting for aftercare instructions.

Whatever they were.

He opened the door, nearly walking into his coworker Chase Zachary.

"You breaking out of this joint?" Chase asked, his coat opened to reveal his uniform and firearm. He didn't have his K-9 partner with him, though.

"Yes."

"You think that's a good idea?"

"It's a better idea than sitting here for another hour. Besides, I need to check on Samson. A DC officer transported him to headquarters."

"Tico is there, too. Vet took a look at both. They're good as gold and eating plenty of good food."

"Have you spoken with Dylan?"

"Just left him. He's fine. Gavin is with him."

"He's not with Virginia?" That worried him, and he was ready to run down the hall, find her and make sure she was okay.

"The little mousy assistant housemother?"

"She's not mousy."

"No." Chase grinned. "I guess it's all in the eye of the beholder. Heard they dug a bullet out of her house. I also heard your house is gone."

"It is." Which was something he hadn't thought too much about. He'd called the Hendersons from the ambulance. They were in Florida for the winter and hadn't seemed overly concerned about their destroyed garage. They hadn't stored anything there, and they had enough insurance and money to cover the loss. They had been concerned about him, though, and had promised to contact their insurance adjuster immediately.

He had renter's insurance and not enough stuff to be all that sorry for the loss of it.

"If you need a place to stay, Erin and I would be happy to have you," Chase offered.

"My landlords said I could stay in their house until the garage is rebuilt. They have an in-law suite in the basement that they're willing to rent me. I'm thinking I may stay at Virginia's for a while, though." He hadn't spoken with her about it, but she needed protection. He had a couple of friends in private security who owed him. He could call one in to help him out.

"You're worried about the guy returning?"

"He blew up a garage, Chase. He's capable of anything."

"You don't know it was him."

"I suspect it."

"Until you prove it—"

"I'm going to proceed with extreme caution. That means making sure he doesn't get another chance to hurt Virginia."

"Morris got the brunt of this one," Chase said grimly. "A broken tibia in his leg. Two broken bones in his foot. He'll be off work for a while."

SEVEN

Laurel's bedroom had been torn apart. Every piece of clothing pulled from every drawer, every pair of shoes tossed from the closet, the place looked as if a tornado had torn through it.

"Looks like he did a pretty good job in here," one of the officers who had escorted Virginia home said.

"I guess so," she said, because she thought that was what he expected, but she didn't feel like replying. She felt like going back to All Our Kids, taking a shower, climbing into bed and forgetting everything for a while.

Her throat hurt, her eyes stung, her body ached. Soot covered her clothes, layered her hair. She'd washed her face at the hospital, but she still thought she could taste soot on her lips.

The fire had almost killed four people.

The guy who'd been breaking into the house, the one who'd crept around while she'd slept, he'd commit murder if he had a chance.

The police had assured her they weren't going to give him that.

She didn't know how they were going to stop him.

He'd already been in the house three times.

It didn't seem as if the threat of being discovered was

keeping him away. Instead of backing off, he'd escalated things. A bomb was what the police were saying. The FBI had been called in and a team was combing through the rubble left when the garage collapsed.

If she looked out the bedroom window, she knew she'd see spotlights gleaming through the darkness, all of them trained on what was left of John's home.

She didn't look.

She didn't want to relive the moment when the house had shaken, the wall had collapsed. If John and the other officer hadn't arrived, she and Officer Morris wouldn't have made it out.

"We're going to have an evidence team go through the room, so don't touch anything," a female officer said, snapping pictures of the mess. "The other rooms weren't touched. I don't think he had time to do more than this. Why don't you go downstairs? Make yourself a cup of tea? Relax while we process everything?"

Because I almost died, she wanted to say. *Because I can't relax until I know that the men who saved me are okay.*

She retreated anyway, walking through the hall and past the room she'd spent two years sleeping in. There were no photos of Kevin displayed in the house. She'd noticed that right away. None of the wedding photos that had once hung from the walls. None of the family photos that Laurel had insisted they have taken every year. It was as if Laurel had tried to erase her grandson from the property. His clothes were still in the bedroom, but other than that, every trace of him was gone.

Funny how time could change memories. Now the things that Virginia had once loved about Kevin had become nothing more than red flags that she'd missed. The lavish gifts, the sweet words, the soft kisses, all of those had been part of the game Kevin had been playing. How far could he go? How much could he push? How deeply could he make Virginia love him?

How much could he hurt her before she ran away?

She guessed they had both figured that out.

She shuddered, the sound of voices drifting up the stairs as she approached the landing. She didn't want to face the people there. Police officers, FBI, fire marshals, members of the Capitol K-9 team, all of them were milling in and out of the house, trying to find answers she didn't think would be found.

She turned around, headed for the back of the house and the door that led up into the attic. It had been locked since she'd arrived, and she hadn't bothered to get the key from Laurel's room. She knew there was another in the vase that sat on a shelf in one of the wall niches that had been added to the house years ago. Before Laurel's time. That's what her grandmother-in-law had told Virginia when she'd given her a tour of the property. Virginia had been blown away by the opulence and grandeur. Everywhere she'd turned there'd been treasures to see. She liked to believe that she hadn't been swayed by all that marrying Kevin offered. She'd loved him deeply at that point, and she'd have been willing to live in a hovel if it had meant being his wife.

She swallowed down bitterness, the acrid scent of smoke swirling around her as she grabbed the vase, dumping the key into her palm. A folded photograph fell out with it.

She carried it with her as she unlocked the attic door and walked up the steps. She turned on a light in the cavernous room. It was quiet there, nothing but the sound of icy rain filling the silence.

Leather trunks still lined the walls, dozens of boxes

interspersed between them. She knew one had Christmas decorations and that another had all Kevin's baby clothes and toys. Several pieces of furniture sat in the center of the finished space—a leather chair that had belonged to Kevin's grandfather, a rocking chair that Laurel had rocked her only son in, the crib that they'd talked about carrying down to the nursery when Virginia and Kevin had children. Every item had a story, but none of the stories had happy endings.

Kevin's mother had given birth to him and then run off with another man. His father had died of a drug overdose a year later, leaving Laurel and her husband to raise their grandson. Now Kevin was gone. Laurel and her husband were gone. Nothing remained of their lives but boxes of things and a house filled with stuff that had never made any of them happy.

Virginia sat in the rocking chair, the key still clutched in one hand, the picture in the other. It hadn't been in the vase before she'd been shot. She knew that for sure. She'd gone into the attic many times during her marriage, creeping up the stairs in the middle of the night to sit in the darkness and pray that her marriage would be healed. that Kevin would be changed.

But God didn't force people to do the right thing, and Kevin's faith had been a facade, lip service to what he'd been raised to believe. There'd been no depth to it, no desire to grow closer to God or to anyone else. Kevin had loved himself. Above all and above everything, getting what he wanted was his primary motivation.

Her eyes burned, but she didn't cry.

It was too late for that, too late to change one thing that had happened.

Footsteps sounded on the attic stairs, but she didn't get up. She didn't have the energy or the motivation to go back downstairs, look through all the rooms that should have been filled with family and love but were filled only with treasures that couldn't fill the holes in her heart.

"Virginia?" John said quietly, stepping into the room, his clothes still covered with soot and ash.

"I'm here," she said, the words hot and dry and hard to speak. There was too much in her throat—too many emotions, too much loss.

"Listening to the sound of the rain on the roof?" he asked, taking a seat in the leather chair beside her. "Or escaping the chaos that is going on downstairs?"

"Neither," she responded. "Both."

He laughed softly, the sound mixing with the rain and the whistle of wind beneath the eaves. "They'll be gone soon."

"I wish I could be."

"You can be. Nothing is holding you here."

"You're wrong." She met his eyes and saw something in his gaze that made her pulse jump. Kindness, compassion, concern, those were things she hadn't ever had from Kevin. Maybe she was greedy for them. Maybe she was searching for something that had been missing from every relationship she'd ever been in. Her parents had been drug addicts, her grandparents had been bitter about having to raise their daughter's child. She'd been shuffled from one home to another for years, each family member a little less caring than the last.

She'd found her way, though. She'd gotten her degree, found a job she'd loved.

Fallen for a guy who could never love her.

She turned away from John, her heart beating frantically.

"You can do whatever you want to do, Virginia," John

said, taking the key from her hand, smoothing out the crescents she'd dug into her palm.

She hadn't felt the pain, but she felt the warm roughness of his fingers. Felt it all the way to her toes.

She tugged away, wiping her palm on her sooty jeans. Even then, she could feel the warmth of his touch.

"What I want is to live my life the same way everyone else does. Without all the baggage and all the memories. I've been trying to do that for years, but it hasn't happened," she muttered, her heart beating a little too fast, her cheeks just a little too warm. "So I'd say you're wrong. I can't do whatever I want. No one really can."

"I guess," he said, slipping the photo from her hand. "That depends on whether or not the person is brave enough to go after what he wants."

"What's that supposed to mean?"

"Just that it's easier to hide from ourselves than it is to hide from anyone else."

"I'm not in the mood for riddles," she murmured.

"No riddle. Just truth. Until you stop feeling guilty about what happened, you're not going to be able to move on."

"I don't feel guilty," she protested, but he was right. She did. If she'd just been smart, strong enough, confident enough none of this ever would have happened. She'd have walked away from Kevin the first time he'd criticized and demeaned her, she'd have left him before the first shove, the first slap, the first threat.

"Like I said, it's a lot easier to hide from ourselves than it is to hide from others." He unfolded the photo and smoothed it out. "What's this?"

"I don't know," she responded, eager to change the subject. Happy to do it. She didn't like that he saw her so clearly, didn't like that she could look in his eyes and see so many things that she'd spent her entire life longing for.

"Looks like a school picture. Kevin's maybe?" He handed it to her, and she studied the class photo. "Fifth grade" was scrolled across the bottom, "Mr. Morrow" and the school year written beneath it. A list of children's names was to the side. Left to right. Front to back.

Not Kevin's fifth-grade photo. Laurel had kept those in a photo album in her closet. Neatly dated, little stick-on arrows pointing to her grandson. Kevin had always been the only kid wearing a tie on picture day. He'd told her once that he'd hated that, told her that he'd hated being raised by people who were too old to understand times changed, cultures changed.

He hadn't had much respect for his grandparents.

He hadn't had much respect for anyone.

"This isn't Kevin's. He would have been in third grade the year it was taken."

"You're sure?"

"Positive. We were the same age, graduated high school the same year. Besides, all the students are listed. His name isn't there."

"You said Laurel didn't have any other grandchildren?"

"Kevin's dad was her only child. He died when he was twenty. A year after Kevin was born."

"He was a young father."

"He and Kevin's mother were pretty heavy into the drug scene. He overdosed. She went to jail, came out clean and went back on the streets a few years later. Lauren said she overdosed when Kevin was ten. He never knew his mother, so I guess it didn't impact him much."

"Where'd you find this?" he asked, taking the photo from her hand again, turning it over as if there might be something on the back that would reveal its secrets.

"In the vase where Laurel kept the spare attic key."

"That's an odd place for a picture."

"It wasn't there when I lived here. She put it there after…"

"It meant something to her, then. Otherwise, she'd have thrown it away. Did you come up here often?"

"A few times a week."

"And you used the key in the vase?"

"Yes."

"Did Laurel know that?"

"She's the one who showed me where it was."

"Then maybe she was trying to show you something else with this. Tell you what—" He stood, offering his hand. "Let's go get Samson. He's at K-9 headquarters. We can use the computers there. See what we can dig up about these kids."

She could have refused, but she was tired of sitting in the old house, listening to her own thoughts. She was tired of feeling trapped by her fears and by the man who seemed determined to make her relive her nightmares.

She took John's hand, allowing herself to be pulled up.

He didn't release his hold as they descended the stairs, and she didn't pull away. She didn't ask herself what that meant. She didn't want to know. She just wanted to find the guy who was terrorizing her, sell Laurel's house and move on with her life.

EIGHT

"No," Virginia said as John pulled into the parking lot at Capitol K-9 headquarters.

He'd outlined his plan for keeping her safe.

She hadn't liked it.

He didn't think many people would like the idea of having strangers living with them twenty-four hours a day, seven days a week.

"The perp isn't playing with a full deck, and he's not playing by any rules any of us can follow."

"I know," she responded, her voice tight, her entire body tight. Muscles taut, expression guarded, she looked ready for a fight.

He didn't plan to give her one. That wasn't the way he operated. Years of helping his mother raise his siblings after their dad passed away had taught him everything he needed to know about winning arguments. Teenagers were tough. Compared to his three younger siblings, Virginia was going to be a piece of cake. She was older, smarter, wiser. And she knew her own mortality, wanted to live, wanted to move on, live life without all the baggage weighing her down.

He'd heard the longing in her voice when they were sitting in the attic. He'd wanted to promise her that everything would be okay, that she'd have what she so desperately wanted.

"If you know, then why are you refusing to let me help you?" he asked.

"Because helping me isn't your responsibility. The DC police are in charge of the case."

"That doesn't relieve me of my obligation to care for my neighbors and my friends," he responded, getting out of the SUV and rounding the vehicle. The storm had passed, but the sky was still gray with thick cloud cover, the blacktop glistening with ice.

Virginia was already out of the vehicle by the time he reached her door. She'd changed before they'd left the house, and the jeans and T-shirt she wore were free of soot, her coat clean. He could still smell smoke in her hair. Or maybe he was smelling it on his clothes and skin. He hadn't bothered trying to find clothes to change into. Everything he owned was in the apartment. He'd be surprised if any of it could be salvaged.

"I don't want to be anyone's obligation," Virginia said as he cupped her elbow and led her to the building.

"Obligation isn't a bad thing."

"It is if you're on the receiving end of it."

"There are a lot worse things to be on the receiving end of—guns, knives. Bombs. Just to name a few." He opened the door and ushered her into headquarters. Someone had put a tree up in the foyer, its boughs covered with ornaments.

"I get that. I just...don't want to owe anyone."

"That's a foolish reason to die, Virginia," he said, the words blunt and a little harsh. He meant them to sound that way, meant for her to understand just how important it was that she have twenty-four-hour protection.

She didn't say anything. Not as they took the elevator up to the third floor. Not as he led the way to his office. Not as she settled into a chair across from his desk.

"I'm going to get Samson. Wait here."

He made it to the door, stepping into the hall when she finally spoke.

"All right," she said quietly. "You and your friend can stay at the house. I'm going to pay you, though. Whatever the going rate is for private security."

That wasn't going to happen.

He didn't tell her that.

Just nodded and walked into the hall.

It didn't take long to retrieve Samson from the kennel. Headquarters was quiet this time of night, most team members either out on guard duty or running patrol. Samson barked happily as John opened the kennel, attached his leash and headed back to the office.

Virginia was standing at the window when he entered the room. She'd pulled her hair into some kind of twist, and he could see her nape, the soft tendrils of hair there and a thick white scar that curved from just behind her ear down into her shirt.

He knew he shouldn't, told himself not to, but he touched the scar, his finger tracing the jagged curves. "Did he do this to you?" he asked, and she turned, meeting his eyes.

"No." She smiled but there was no pleasure in it. "I did it to myself. I was six and determined to find my mother. I tried to climb from a second-story window into an old oak tree. It didn't work out."

"Where was your mom?"

"On the streets somewhere. She was clean for most of the first six years of my life. Then…" She shrugged. "She gave in to the cravings, and the drugs became way more important than I was."

"I'm sorry," he said, and she smiled again.

"I spent a lot of time being sorry, too, then I almost died and I realized that I hadn't done anything to make her leave and that I never could have been enough to make her stay. Once I understood that, it didn't hurt so much."

"You've had a rocky road, haven't you?" he asked, touching her cheek, letting his palm rest against her cool skin.

"Not as rocky as some people. How about you?" she asked as she bent to scratch Samson's head.

"My road has been pretty smooth," he responded. His father's death had been difficult, but his family had had support and love from friends, family and the community. Losing his brother had been devastating, but he'd had other siblings to think about, his mother to focus on. And he'd had his faith. It told him that goodbye wasn't forever, that he'd see his father, brother and grandfather again. That didn't make the loss easy, but it did make it bearable.

"Did you grow up in the suburbs with a mother and father and a couple of siblings? Did you eat meals together every night and go to church every Sunday?"

"Something like that. Until my father died. Then things got a little more difficult."

"I'm sorry, John. Was he ill?"

"He was a police officer. Killed in the line of duty. We lost my grandfather and brother the same way."

"Your road wasn't nearly as smooth as you made it out to be." She touched his wrist, and he captured her hand and tugged her a step closer, because there was something about her that made him want to look a little longer, see a little more of who she was.

"Every road has a few bumps," he said, because it

was true, and he didn't waste much time feeling bad because he'd hit a few. "Now, how about we take another look at the picture?"

The picture. Right.

Virginia had been so busy looking into John's eyes, she'd forgotten that they had a reason for being in his office. One that didn't include long conversations about their pasts, about their families, about the things they'd been through.

He sat behind the desk, and she took the seat across from him, pulling the photo out of her coat pocket and flattening it against the desk. "There must be someone Laurel knew here. She didn't keep things just to keep them."

"You're sure about that?" he asked. "Because from the look of the house, I'd say she liked to collect lots of things."

"She did, but everything she collected had value or meaning. She never kept something just to keep it." As a matter of fact, Laurel had had a story for every item in the house. Some of the stories had been passed down to her, some she'd lived. She might have joined the Johnson family through marriage, but she'd embraced the history of it with a zeal that Virginia was never able to match. "If she kept this, she did it because it was important to her."

"Important how?" he asked, and she studied the photo, scanning the names, the teacher, the first row of kids, the second row.

"I don't…" Her voice trailed off as she got to the end of the third row. A boy stood unsmiling just a little apart from the group. He had dark hair. Kevin had been blond when he was in grade school. It was the face that made her pause. The high cheekbones, the cleft chin, the eyes.

He looked so much like Kevin had at that age, they could have been brothers.

"What's wrong?" John leaned forward, his hand brushing Virginia's as he turned the photo so that he could see it more clearly.

"This," she responded, jabbing at the boy. "Could be Kevin. Except for the dark hair."

"What's his name?"

She ran her finger along the list of kids until she landed on the correct one. "Luke Miller."

The name tripped off her tongue, and her pulse jumped. "That's the name of the guy—"

"Laurel visited in prison," he finished, lifting the photo, eyeing the boy who'd turned into a man who'd spent more than a third of his life in jail.

"She also helped him get his college education," she said quietly.

"I wonder what else she did for him?" John murmured, turning on his computer, typing something in. He printed a page, then passed it over to her. "Look familiar?" he asked.

Her blood ran cold as she looked into the face of the man she'd seen on the stairs. Light brown hair. Hazel eyes. Prison orange.

A mug shot?

"This is the guy I saw," she confirmed, and John typed something else.

"According to our records, he's living in Suitland, Maryland, in a halfway house for recovering addicts. Last time he checked in with his parole officer was last week."

"Suitland isn't far," she said, and he shook his head.

"Twenty-minute drive without traffic. He could be leaving and returning without garnering too much attention. Or he could have walked out and not returned."

"Walked out and gone to Laurel's house, you mean? Squatted there because he knew she wasn't returning?"

"It's a good possibility." He took out his cell phone and texted someone. "I'm contacting Margaret Meyer. She runs Capitol K-9. If anyone can get several law enforcement entities working together, she can. Hopefully we can have this guy back behind bars in a few hours."

"From your lips to God's ears," she replied, walking back to the window that looked out over the parking lot.

They were in the middle of DC, and the lights from dozens of buildings glowed through the darkness. Wreaths hung from the streetlights. Red Christmas bows decorated a fence that surrounded the parking area. The holidays were approaching, and the world was preparing. All Virginia wanted to do was hide.

"It's going to be okay, Virginia," John said, his arm sliding around her waist. He didn't offer a million words to try to reassure her. He didn't tell her all the reasons why her fears were unfounded. He just stood beside her, the soft silence of the building, the warmth of his arm on her waist oddly reassuring.

"I'm not hanging my hat on that," she said quietly, and he chuckled.

"Ever the optimist, huh?"

"I prefer to be realistic."

"Realistic and hopeful. That's the best combination."

Hopeful? It had been a long time since she'd felt that, years since hope had bubbled up and spilled out into her life. She wasn't sure she remembered what it felt like. Sunrise, maybe? The first day of a new year? Christmas morning with presents under the tree? Life stretched out before her, a hundred possibilities there for the choosing?

Only she'd chosen Kevin. Her biggest and most lasting mistake. Her chest itched where the bullet had entered, the old wound healed over now, but still there. Every time she looked in the mirror, she was reminded of just how lousy her decision-making ability could be, and each time she was reminded, she vowed not to make the same mistake again.

"I'm not sure I remember what hope feels like," she admitted, the words spilling out. "I only remember what it's like to have it crushed."

"Disappointments are inevitable," he said, turning her so that they were facing each other, his gaze solemn, his hands soft as they cupped her shoulders. "Being destroyed by them is not."

"I haven't been destroyed," she responded, because she'd gone on, she'd made a good life for herself.

He studied her for a moment, his blue eyes as sharp and crisp as a fall morning.

"No. I guess you haven't. Just make sure you haven't been diminished by it, either. Come on. My friend is going to meet us at the house. He can run guard duty while you and I dig around, see if we can figure out what the connection is between Laurel and Luke."

"They must be related," she said as they walked into the corridor, Samson trotting beside them. "Laurel believed in family above almost anything else. If Luke was part of the family, she'd have done anything to help him."

"If that's true, there will be evidence of it. We just have to find it."

She would rather go back to All Our Kids. She'd rather forget all about the house, the Kevin look-alike, the secrets that Laurel had obviously been keeping.

She'd rather, but she doubted that would keep her safe, so she allowed herself to be led through the building and back out into the wintry night.

NINE

Five days cooped up in the house with two men was starting to get to Virginia. Much as she wanted to enjoy her extra time off, she couldn't. The walls were closing in around her, the itemized lists of antiques and collectibles growing longer every day, because that's what she spent most of her time doing—going through every drawer, every closet, every cupboard and shelf, writing down Laurel's treasures.

She still hadn't found anything that would link Luke Miller to the Johnson family. The police hadn't been able to find a connection, either. Luke had grown up a few miles from the Johnson's posh neighborhood. His mother had been in and out of his life, and he'd been raised by his maternal grandmother in a community of low-income apartments. He'd been smart enough and driven enough to earn a scholarship to the prestigious school that Kevin had attended.

Maybe that's how Laurel had met him?

She wasn't sure and didn't have the freedom to leave the house and go searching for answers.

She was trapped like a rat.

For her own safety. That's what Gavin had said when he'd told her that she needed to stay put until Luke was apprehended. She'd planned to return to work at the beginning of the week. Instead, she was living in the one place she'd vowed to never return to.

"Irony," she said, and Samson lifted his head, cocking it to the side. John and another Capitol K-9 officer were having a meeting of the minds in the kitchen. Dylan seemed like a nice guy. That didn't mean she wanted to spend the better part of five days hanging around him.

Unfortunately, there hadn't been any leads. Luke had walked out of the halfway house and dropped off the grid.

Virginia hoped that he'd drop back on soon, because she wanted to get back to her life. She had Christmas cookies to bake with the kids, a house to decorate, a tree to put up. All the little traditions that she and Cassie had put into place when they'd begun working together needed to be revisited for the sake of the children who'd been with them long-term. Some of those kids had never had traditions, had never experienced constancy. They craved routine and familiarity like other kids craved ice cream or sweets.

Right now, they were missing Virginia desperately.

She heard it in their voices every time she called All Our Kids to check in—worry tinged with betrayal. She'd always been there for them. Now she wasn't.

That hurt them and it hurt her.

The sun had set hours ago, and she'd called just before the youngest of the foster kids' bedtime. She'd said goodnight to each child, heard various renditions of the same theme: *When are you coming home? Why do you have to be away for so long?*

How could she explain without worrying kids who already worried too much?

She'd made it simple. Just told them that cleaning out

the house was taking a long time. Eventually that excuse wasn't going to work. Eventually, she needed to return.

Eventually meaning sooner rather than later.

Too bad she didn't have any control over things.

She scowled, yanking open the bottom drawer of the dresser that sat against the wall in the blue room. Laurel had always called it that, and Virginia had never figured out why. It was the brightest room in the house. Not a speck of blue in any of the decorations. No dark wood furniture or paneling. The wallpaper soft yellow with tiny white roses sprinkled across it. White wainscoting covered the lower portion of the walls. Even the furniture was white—the canopy bed sitting in the middle of the wood floor.

"It's a little too much, if you ask me," she said, and Samson huffed, setting his head back down on his paws. He'd prefer to be with John, but he'd been commanded to stay with her. Something John did every time he had a meeting to attend or business that needed doing.

John…

He was turning into a problem.

No matter how much she tried not to like him, no matter how many times she told herself that he was just a guy helping her out, a guy who would disappear from her life as soon as Luke had been apprehended, she couldn't stop her pulse from leaping every time he entered the room, couldn't stop the warmth that settled in her heart every time she looked in his eyes.

He was…special.

Not in the phony, fake way Kevin had been. John was exactly what he seemed to be—strong, determined, caring.

He'd brought a box of Christmas decorations the previous day, telling her that it was time to make the place a little more festive. What he'd really been trying to do was get her mind off Luke, Kevin, Laurel—a dozen things she could do nothing about.

She'd wanted to ask him to take the decorations away, but she'd looked into his blue eyes, seen the compassion and concern there, and she'd found herself hanging a garland from the banister and bows from fireplace mantels.

"He's going to be a problem," she said as she lifted a stack of tablecloths from the drawer.

"Who?" John said, his voice so unexpected, she jumped.

"You," she responded honestly, jotting a note on her tablet—*Five lace tablecloths. Old. Handmade?*

"Should I be flattered or chastised?" he asked, settling onto the floor beside her, a soft smile easing the hard lines of his face.

"That depends."

"On?"

"Whether you like being a problem."

"That depends," he replied, taking the tablet from her hand and setting it on the dresser.

"On?"

"What kind of problem we're talking about." He stood and pulled her to her feet, his dark jeans and dark T-shirt brand-new. He hadn't shopped for them, had barely left the house the past few days. Coworkers had delivered the things he'd needed, bringing by several items that had been salvaged from the fire.

Mostly, John's belongings had been destroyed.

He'd never once complained. Just gone through the process of replacing them. Not an easy task when he spent every moment of his days babysitting Virginia.

She frowned, closing the drawer and walking to the lone painting that hung on the wall. It was the only decoration. Unlike every other room in the house, the blue room was devoid of knickknacks and collectibles. Aside from the one painting, nothing hung from the wall. Everything was simple and elegant, understated and pretty.

"You're the kind of problem—" she began as she lifted the painting from its hook. Beneath it was one of three wall safes that had been installed decades ago. She'd already been through the other two "—that could break a girl's heart if she let it."

There. She'd said it. What she'd been thinking for days. If she let herself, she could fall for John. If that happened, she'd end up hurt. It was inevitable, right? Because she had no ability to choose things that were good for her, men who would treat her well.

Hadn't she proven that?

"To break someone's heart," he said as she turned the combination lock. "I'd have to do something to hurt her."

"To break someone's heart," she responded as she opened the safe, "you'd simply have to walk away."

"Are we talking about you, Virginia?" He turned her so that they were face-to-face, and she couldn't help looking straight into his eyes. "Because once I commit to someone, I don't walk away."

"We're not committed. Not even close," she pointed out.

"But we could be. If we let ourselves head in that direction."

"I've made too many mistakes, and I—"

"Don't trust yourself enough to know you've learned from them?" he asked, his voice a little rough, his finger gentle as he traced a line along her jaw and down to the pulse point in her neck. His finger rested there, and she knew he could feel how quickly her heart was beating.

"Maybe. Or maybe I'm just afraid of being hurt. I'm afraid of finding out that something I've pinned my hopes on is just a facade, a trick of the light and of my mind."

She turned back to the safe, reaching blindly for a pile of papers, her eyes burning with tears that shouldn't have been there.

She'd cried herself out years ago, but a tear slipped down her cheek anyway, dropped onto the papers she was holding.

"Don't cry," John said softly, pulling her into his arms, his hands smoothing her hair, resting on her back. She should have stepped away. She knew she should have, but she burrowed in closer, let her head rest against his chest, let her arms slide around his waist.

This was where she wanted to be. Right here. With this man. It didn't matter that they were in a house she'd spent years hating. It didn't matter that she'd lived a dozen nightmares in the room down the hall, in the kitchen below, in the hallway and on the porch. It didn't matter, because John filled the dark places, made her feel strong when she'd only ever felt weak.

"It's going to be okay," he said. "I promise."

"Promises are a dime a dozen," she replied, and he chuckled.

"We really do need to work on your optimism." He stepped back, wiped the moisture from her cheeks. "Anything interesting in that safe?"

"Just papers." She glanced down at what she was holding—a birth certificate. The name scrawled across it made her pulse jump.

"It's his," she said, holding it out to John. "Luke Miller."

This was it.

Exactly what they needed to prove the connection between Luke and Laurel. Birth certificates didn't lie, and this one listed Ryan Johnson as Luke's father. His mother was a woman whose name John had never heard mentioned—Alice Randal. Both were dead. Not Kevin's mother.

"Ryan was your father-in-law?" he asked, and Virginia nodded.

"He must have had another son a few years before Kevin was born."

"Laurel never mentioned it." She frowned, tucking a few strands of hair behind her ear. "Neither did Kevin."

"They knew. Or Laurel did. Looks like she was paying good money for the woman to keep quiet." John set the birth certificate on the dresser and took the stack of papers from Virginia's hands. Paternity test results, stacks of cashed checks written out to the woman who'd been listed as Luke's mother. Another birth certificate for a baby born nearly fifty years ago. A little girl. Her death certificate was right behind it.

"It also looks like Laurel had another child," he said.

"She never mentioned that, either." She reached for the death certificate, her hands shaking. "Poor Laurel. So many secrets."

"Some of them even more upsetting." He held up a Polaroid photo of a woman, her face battered—eye black, lip swollen.

"Laurel," Virginia murmured, taking the photo from his hand. "She always said her husband was the best thing that had ever happened to her."

"Maybe she believed that, but there are several more. Dated." He handed her one that showed the same woman, blue and black smudges on her neck, eye blackened, lip cracked and bleeding. Someone had beaten her black-and-blue, and someone else had shot the Polaroid photo documenting the abuse that had happened decades ago. "She was keeping record of the abuse. Maybe she'd planned to go to the police."

"Maybe." She studied the photo, her eyes dark with

sadness. "I believed her when she said her husband was a wonderful guy. She showed me all the things he'd bought her and told me dozens of stories about vacations and spa days and flowers for no reason."

"Flowers as apologies. Gifts to say 'I'm sorry,'" he said without thinking, and she winced, obviously familiar with the pattern, with the thought process that allowed an intelligent, independent woman to be pulled into an abusive relationship. "When did he die?" he asked, changing the subject because he hated to see the darkness in her eyes.

"When Kevin was ten. He had a stroke." She worried her lower lip, lifted another Polaroid photo from the stack he was holding. "She stayed in this house, told everyone what a wonderful marriage she'd had, made the lies bigger and brighter, made the past so much more beautiful than it was."

"Maybe it was the only way she could survive," he said gently, and she nodded, the gesture stiff.

"Maybe so." Her shoulders slumped, and she glanced around the room. "No wonder she called this the blue room. She had a lot of sadness stored in that safe."

"I'm sorry," he said, sitting beside her, his fingers playing in the ends of her silky hair. She had beautiful hair, beautiful skin, the kind of soft prettiness that would only grow more lovely with age.

He could imagine her at fifty, sixty, seventy, could imagine himself, still looking in her face, still seeing her quiet determination, her strength.

"Me, too. If she'd been more open about her past, Kevin might have learned from the mistakes of his grandfather, or I might have learned from hers. But... she wasn't, and it's all water under the bridge. There's nothing that anyone can do about any of it."

"You're wrong there," he said. "He's part of the past,

and a big part of the present, and there is most definitely something that can be done about him. He can be tossed back in jail. You're certain Kevin never mentioned him?"

"Positive."

"Do you think he knew? Or maybe the better question is—do you think Laurel told him?"

"Based on all the other secrets she kept, I'd say she didn't. Laurel liked things tidy and nice. The idea of her son having an illegitimate child was probably difficult to swallow. Finding out he'd had two? I don't think she'd want anyone to know that. That doesn't mean Kevin didn't know. He kept secrets, too. I guess it was a family heritage." She smiled, but there was no humor in it.

Samson stood, growling quietly as he paced to the window and stood on his haunches, looking out into the yard.

"What is it, boy?" John stood and took a step toward the window, calling for the dog to heel. He didn't want Samson anywhere near the window if the suspect was outside. They knew Luke was armed, they knew he was dangerous. They knew he wouldn't hesitate to kill if he had the chance.

Samson retreated, still barking.

"Cease," John commanded, the sudden silence thick with something—tension, danger.

Downstairs, Dylan's dog sounded an alarm.

That was it. All John needed to hear. He called for backup, snagging Virginia's hand and pulling her into the hall.

Glass shattered. The blue room suddenly filled with smoke.

Something rolled across the floor skittering toward them as Samson howled.

"Get down," John shouted, tackling Virginia to the floor as the world exploded.

TEN

Chaos.

Dogs barking. Someone shouting. Darkness. Smoke.

Something nudged her cheek. A cold nose, a furry face.

Samson?

Virginia tried to get up, but John was pressing her down, his body a solid weight holding her in place.

"Wait," he said as she struggled to sit.

"The place could go up in flames."

"There's no fire. That was a smoke canister of some sort," he said. "He's just trying to draw us out."

"He's doing a good job of it," she said, pushing against John's chest. "I want out."

"We leave, and we'll walk right into the line of fire."

"We can't just—"

He pulled her to her feet. "*We* aren't going to do anything. Go in Laurel's room. Lock the door. Stay away from the windows."

He shouted the instructions as he dragged her down the hall. The smoke was nearly gone, just tiny wisps of it still swirling through the air.

"You're not going after him?" she said, fear making her voice hollow.

"I've been waiting for this chance for days." He opened the door and nudged her in. "I'm taking this guy down."

"What if he takes you down first?" she asked, all the old fears gone, all the nightmares disappearing in one moment of clarity—the past didn't matter, the pain didn't matter. The old hurts? They didn't matter, either.

All that mattered was John staying safe. All that mattered was him walking through the door again and again, smiling at her, telling her that she needed to be more optimistic. All that mattered was seeing where hope took them, seeing where trust led, seeing what the future would bring if she stopped being too afraid to grab hold of it, believe in it.

"Don't go," she said, grabbing his hand, trying to pull him into the room with her. "He's crazy. He could kill you and not blink an eye while he was doing it."

"I've got Samson, Dylan and his dog. We're better armed and better prepared than Luke."

"But—"

"I already called for help, Virginia. Backup will be here any minute.

"I—"

"Enough," he said quietly. "We're wasting time we don't have. You've got to trust me, Virginia. I know what I'm doing."

She looked into his eyes, had a million words she wanted to say. Only a few mattered, only a few could be the start of what they were going to build together.

"I do," she finally said, and he smiled, dropping a quick kiss to her lips.

"Stay away from the windows," he reminded her as he pulled the door closed, and then he was gone, and she was alone, fear pulsing through her veins, hope filling her heart.

* * *

Samson ran for the back staircase, barking ferociously. They hit the landing and raced into the kitchen. Dylan was there, Tico on his lead, lunging at the back door.

"He's out there," Dylan said grimly. "I caught a glimpse of him near the tree line at the back edge of the property. Too far for me to get a good shot, or I would have taken it."

"We get him now, or this could drag on forever. You stay here. I'll take Samson out."

"It's your show," Dylan said, his eyes trained on the back door. "I suggest you go out the front, though. The guy is probably packing."

No doubt about that. John was prepared, though. He knew what he was up against, knew that Gavin and Chase were only minutes away. Luke Miller was going to be sorry he'd come back. He was going to be sorry that he'd ever decided to make a play for Laurel's property.

That had to be what this was—an effort to get rid of Virginia so that Luke could inherit. It was a crazy plan, but Luke seemed like the kind of guy who just might think it would work. He'd been in and out of juvenile detention from the time he was thirteen until he was arrested at eighteen. Went to jail three times before he was put away long-term.

The guy had an inflated sense of his own abilities, and he seemed to think he could stay one step ahead of law enforcement.

It wasn't going to happen.

John opened the front door and eased outside. Samson was alert but relaxed, no sign that Luke was anywhere nearby.

"Find!" John commanded, and the German shepherd

rounded the side of the house. John hesitated at the corner, letting the dog get a good whiff of the air.

Nothing.

Had Luke retreated?

That would be the best-case scenario.

And the worst.

He wanted to take Luke down, put him in jail, make sure he never got out.

"Find," he urged Samson, and the dog trotted across the yard, then sprinted toward their old apartment.

Nothing was left of it but a pile of rubble.

They raced out onto the street. A dark car was parked a few houses up. Empty, but Samson spent a few minutes sniffing the door, scratching at the windows.

Luke's ride. It had to be.

That meant the suspect was still in the area, still trying to fulfill whatever mission he'd set for himself.

Kill Virginia?

Take something from the house?

Whatever it was, John planned to stop him.

He called in the location of the car, updated Gavin and Chase on his location and put Samson back on the scent. They moved toward the park, darkness pressing in on every side. No moonlight. The clouds were too heavy, the air thick with moisture. A few flakes of snow fell as Samson led the way through the empty park. Nothing moved. No animals. No people.

Behind them, a branch cracked, and Samson let out a long, low growl, turning sharply toward the sound.

"Come out of there!" John called, knowing the perp was close, that he was somewhere in the darkness of the trees. He stayed low, keeping foliage between him and whatever Samson could sense.

Samson growled again, his body tense, his scruff raised.

John reached for his lead, unhooking it from Samson's collar. "Come out, or I'll release my dog."

Nothing.

No movement.

No hint that someone was there.

Someone was. John felt the danger as clearly as he felt the cold air.

"I said—"

A flash of light cut off the words. Seconds later, he heard the gun's report. The bullet slammed into a tree a few yards from where they stood.

John released his hold on Samson's collar. The dog was well trained, he knew what to do. He needed no command, just leaped through the foliage, barreling toward the gunman.

Seconds later, Samson snarled, the sound a clear indication that he had the suspect in sight.

A man yelled, and the gun fired again, the bullet flying into the tree canopy.

Success.

John knew it, could hear the man's frantic cries for help.

He ran toward the sound, found Samson standing over the suspect, the guy's arm in his mouth.

"Release!" John commanded, pulling his gun, aiming it at the perp. "Don't move."

"I wasn't going to," the guy said, his face pale in the beam of John's flashlight, his eyes dark rather than hazel, his skin tan rather than light.

Black hair. A tattoo over his eye.

Not Luke Miller. This was a kid. Maybe nineteen. His gaze darted back and forth—his jerky movements and pockmarked skin telling a story of addiction that John didn't have time to read.

"Where's Miller?" he demanded, yanking the kid to his feet and frisking him. The gun he'd used lay a few feet away, and John cuffed the perp before retrieving it.

"I ain't talking."

"John!" Someone called, the sound reverberating through the darkness. Gavin. Chase was probably with him, both of them thinking they were chasing after Luke.

Which left Dylan alone at the house with Virginia.

He could handle himself, but John didn't like the feeling he was getting. The one that said he'd made a mistake, that he'd walked right into a trap set by a madman.

"Here!" he called, shoving the kid back the way they'd come.

"You're not taking me back to that house," he spat, struggling against John's hold.

"That's exactly where we're going."

"No way, man!" the kid whined. "I don't want to die."

That was it. All the words John needed to hear. Gavin was just a few feet ahead, Glory on lead, Chase a few yards behind. He shoved the kid their way.

"There's trouble back at Virginia's house," he said. "Call it in and take care of this kid."

"What kind of trouble?" Chase asked, moving in beside him as he raced back the way they'd come.

"I don't know, but—"

His voice trailed off.

Smoke was billowing up from somewhere just in front of them, the puffy tendrils of it dark against the clouds.

His heart raced, adrenaline pouring through him.

"Fire," he shouted, running back toward the house, his feet pounding on grass and then pavement, every nerve in his body screaming for him to hurry.

The trap had been set.

Send in a ringer, get one guard to leave the property, lure the other one out.

So much easier to take out one person than two, so much simpler to get to the person you wanted if you made her come to you.

If the house was on fire, Dylan would have to bring Virginia outside.

Luke was waiting there, ready to fire a shot as soon as they exited the building.

John knew it.

He tried to call Dylan, warn him, but his friend didn't pick up. Were there other officers nearby? Someone who could stop what was about to happen?

John couldn't count on it.

Please, God, let me get there in time.

The prayer filled his head, gave wings to his feet.

God, please, he prayed again as he raced out of the park and into the street beyond.

ELEVEN

Smoke filled the room, filled her lungs, the heat of the fire lapping at the floorboards making her want to open the window, climb out into the wintry cold.

She didn't. Couldn't.

She had to find Dylan, make sure he was okay.

She didn't hear his dog, didn't hear him, could hear nothing but the roar of the blaze that seemed to be sweeping up the exterior wall of the house.

A crack. A whoosh.

Heat. Flames.

All of it had happened too quickly for thought, too quickly for panic.

She felt the bedroom door—cool to the touch—and opened it.

There was less smoke in the hall, less heat.

"Dylan?" she called.

No response. She ran to the bathroom, grabbed a towel and soaked it.

She draped it over her head and shoulders, running for the back stairs.

No sign of the fire there. The house was eerily silent, the kitchen dark.

She crept into the room, cold air blowing in through the open door.

Someone was outside.

Waiting.

She could see the shadow of his head, the outline of his shoulders.

Not Dylan. This guy was too narrow, too short.

Not John, either.

She was terrified to move forward, terrified to go back.

"You may as well come out," someone called in a sing-song voice that made her skin crawl. "I've already taken care of your friend and his mutt. There's no one here to help you. It's just the two of us, so let's talk about what I want." A lie. She knew it. There was no way Dylan and Tico had been 'taken care of.' They were somewhere, waiting to step in. She just had to trust that they'd do it before Luke acted.

"What do you want?" she asked, her voice shaky.

She didn't move forward, didn't dare put herself within reach of Luke.

"Everything that belongs to me. All that is rightfully mine. This house. The money. All of it."

"The house you're burning down?" she asked, hoping to distract him, to keep him talking until help arrived.

And it would arrive.

She had to believe that, had to trust that John had realized what was happening and was heading back toward the house.

"Barely a flame, Ginny," Luke called in that same singsongy tone. "The wood and paint on this place are fire retardant. Laurel had a deep fear of flames. Didn't you know that?"

"No."

"I did. She told me all about it when she came to visit me in prison. Amazing what a little guilt will do. Opens up the floodgates, makes people reveal things they normally wouldn't. She told me that she'd had the whole place painted with something that would prevent a fire from taking hold. I checked into that before I came up with my plan. Just to make sure she was telling the truth."

"She didn't feel that guilty. She left the property to me," she said, purposely rocking the boat, purposely prodding him.

She needed to keep him talking, and she needed to keep him outside.

Could she get to the door? Close it before he had time to react?

"She felt plenty guilty," he growled. "But she felt guiltier about raising another wife beater. Third in the line, you know. The old man beat the stuffing out of my mom when she was pregnant with me. That's why they didn't marry. That's why I was born into poverty and squalor instead of excess. She should have just taken the beatings and let me have what was rightfully mine. It would have saved us all a lot of trouble."

"You're crazy."

"Am I?" He stepped into the kitchen, and her blood ran cold.

It was Kevin again, standing in the bedroom, the gun in hand.

You can't leave me. Won't leave me. Not now. Not ever.

She'd seen insanity in his eyes that day. She'd known she was going to die.

She saw it now, felt the same mind-numbing fear.

She had to act, but she didn't know which way to go, what way to turn.

"What do you want?" she managed to say.

"Your signature." He pulled a paper from his pocket,

the gun still pointed in her direction. "It says everything goes to me if you die."

"There's no way anyone will ever believe that."

"So?" He laughed. "It's the irony I want. You handing everything over to me right before you die. It's perfect justice."

"Even if you never get a penny?" She eased toward the kitchen counter, the knife block that was there. If she could grab one, she could defend herself.

"I don't want money. I want you to suffer like I've suffered. Simple as that, Ginny. You took my brother from me before I had time to really get to know him. You took my grandmother from me. You took my inheritance. My life. Everything that should have been mine."

"Nothing in this house is yours. It was Laurel's, and I had nothing to do with her death. I hadn't spoken to her in eight years when she died."

"She died from a broken heart. She lost everything. You did that to her."

"I didn't—"

"Shut up!" he screamed, rage contorting his face. She'd seen the same in Kevin's face too many times to count, and every time, she'd run from it, cowered from it, tried desperately to assuage it.

Not this time.

There was nowhere to go. Nothing she could do but fight.

She lunged forward, slamming into him as the pantry door flew open.

A dog snarled and snapped. A man shouted.

Feet pounded on the back deck.

She heard it all, felt the cold metal of a gun pressed to her temple.

"Stop!" Luke screamed, and the world went silent.

Not a sound from Dylan, who'd jumped out of the pantry and stood with his gun trained at Luke. Not a sound from his K-9 partner.

"Don't do anything stupid, Miller," John barked.

He stood in the doorway, his firearm out, Samson growling beside him.

A frozen tableau of men and dogs and insanity, the gun still pressed to her temple.

"One move and she dies. You hear me?" Luke said.

She caught a glimpse of someone moving outside.

Chase or Gavin heading to the front of the house?

Probably, but they'd get there too late.

She could have told them that.

Could have told John that doing what Luke said wasn't going to save her. She didn't say anything, though. Didn't dare speak as Luke dragged her toward the hallway.

She thought she knew where they were heading. To the front yard. To the spot where she'd collapsed. To the place where Kevin had died.

Irony to die where her husband had killed himself.

She met John's eyes, saw determination there, knew that he would risk everything to save her.

She couldn't let him die.

Couldn't let anyone else be hurt.

The gun was still there, pressed to her temple, the metal cold and hard, but Luke was distracted, his grip loosening as he tried to keep everyone under control.

This was going to be her only chance.

She had to take it.

She slammed her elbow into Luke's side, letting all her weight fall against his arm.

Someone shouted. A gun exploded.

Pain seared her temple, stole her thoughts, and then she was falling, Luke's laughter ringing in her ears, mixing with memories of Kevin's voice, his shouts, his tears and moans and apologies, all of it there together, filling her head, pounding through her blood, carrying her away.

John tucked his revolver back into the holster, every cell in his body focused, every bit of who he was dedicated to one thing—keeping Virginia alive.

He'd seen the intention in her eyes a split second before she'd acted; he hadn't had time to tell her to stop, to wait, to let the plan play out—Chase and Gavin flanking Luke, taking him down from behind while John distracted him.

Only Virginia had acted first, and now she was lying on the ground, blood seeping from her head.

Luke lay a few feet away.

Dead.

John had taken the shot and had hit his target, taken him out with one bullet to the heart. He knew it. Couldn't find it in himself to feel more than rage for what Luke had done, what he'd been trying to do. The sorrow would come later. For the life that was lost, but not for the man who was gone. Luke had brought this on himself, and it had ended the way he'd wanted—with blood and death and violence.

John leaned over Virginia, Samson nosing in, trying to lick Virginia's cheek.

"Down," John said, pulling off his coat, pressing the sleeve to the seeping wound.

His hand was steady as he felt for her pulse, but his soul was shaking, everything in him shouting that he had to save her.

"Don't worry," she said, groggily, her eyes still closed. "It's just a flesh wound."

"This—" he said, wiping at the blood, relief coursing

through him. A millimeter in either direction and the bullet would have gone through the skull and into the brain, killing her almost instantly "—is more than a flesh wound."

"Probably," she responded, finally opening her eyes. "But I've always wanted to say that."

That made him smile.

She made him smile.

"I guess you've achieved your life goal, then," he said, applying pressure to the wound.

She winced, but didn't complain. "Luke?"

"Gone."

"I think I should be sorry for that," she said, her words slurred, her eyes hazy. She had a concussion at best. A fractured skull at worst.

She was alive, though, and that was something John would be forever thankful for.

"You will be one day. But not now. Not after everything that happened."

"Thanks for saving me," she said, as an ambulance crew moved in.

"You saved yourself, Virginia."

"No," she insisted, grabbing his hand when the paramedic tried to shoo him away. "You did. You made me believe in things I'd given up on. You made me hope for things I'd stopped believing I could have."

"What things?" he asked, brushing hair from her cheek, his heart aching with a love he'd never expected to feel. His life had been too busy, too devoted to his siblings, then his job. He hadn't had room for anything else until Virginia had come along.

She fit perfectly. In his life. His heart.

He wouldn't give that up.

Wouldn't turn away from it.

"Happy endings," she murmured, as the paramedics lifted her onto the gurney.

Her eyes were closed, but she clutched his hand, refusing to release him as they carried her out the back door.

She fell silent as they rounded the house, her hand going slack, her hold loosening.

He climbed into the ambulance, settled into a seat the paramedic indicated and nodded at Gavin, who was standing at the back of the ambulance, Samson on the lead beside him.

"I'll take him to my place," he said, and John nodded. "I'll call as soon as I hear something."

"Trust me. That won't be necessary. Cassie is looking for someone to come sit with the kids. We'll be at the hospital as soon as she finds someone."

"No," Virginia mumbled. "That isn't necessary. Tell her to stay home."

"That would be like telling you to stop caring about your kids," Gavin responded gruffly. "Stay with her. Those are direct orders from Cassie," he said to John.

There was no need for the orders, because there was no way John was leaving Virginia's side.

The ambulance doors closed, and the vehicle raced toward the hospital. Virginia didn't speak, didn't moan, barely seemed to be breathing.

"Virginia?" he said, touching her cheek.

"I have a pretty bad headache, so this isn't the best time to talk," she responded.

"Too bad, I wanted to hear more about the things I helped you believe in."

"You just want to keep me awake, because you're afraid I'll lose consciousness and drift away for good," she accused.

"Guilty as charged," he said, and she opened her eyes and met his gaze, offering a soft smile.

"Don't worry, John. I'm not going anywhere." She reached out, touched his cheeks. "Not when I've finally found what I've spent my life looking for."

"What's that?"

"A place to belong. Someone to belong with. A chance for something that can last. I thought I had that with Kevin, but it was just a dream that I created. There was no substance to it."

"There will be plenty of substance to us," he promised, and her smile broadened.

"We'll see how you hold up under the pressure."

"What pressure?"

"Of Christmas shopping with a bunch of kids, of baking cookies with little people under your feet. Decorating with babies on your hip and a toddler whining for a candy cane. It's a busy month at All Our Kids, and I can't wait to get back to it." Her eyes drifted closed again, the smile failing away, a tinge of pink on her cheeks. "But I guess I'm getting ahead of myself. You'll probably be—"

"Doing all those things with you," he said, cutting her off, because he could see himself with her and the foster kids she worked with. He could picture Christmas in the house filled with children who needed more than gifts and treats. Who needed love, affection, constancy.

"Really?" She took his hand, lifted it to her mouth and kissed his knuckles. "Then you're a brave man, John. Much braver than I thought."

He laughed at that, squeezing her hand gently.

She had a long recovery ahead of her. He knew that, and he planned to be with her every step of the way. Through Christmas, the New Year, beyond. That was what commitment meant, it was what love meant, it was what he felt every time he looked into her eyes.

He wanted more of that. For himself. For her. He wanted to offer Virginia all the things she'd been searching for, all the things she deserved. Happiness. Joy. Security.

Love.

She seemed willing to ride things out, see where they led, what the two of them could create together. That was a beginning, and he thought it would also be an end—of walking the road alone, of forging his path without any commitments or obligations to anyone but himself. Just his job, his dog, his friends, his neighbors. No deep connections that could mold the heart and shape the soul.

He hadn't realized how much he'd longed for something more until God had set it in his life, shown him how much he was missing out on.

Snow was falling as the ambulance pulled into the hospital parking lot, heavy white flakes that coated the ground and seemed to bring a sense of renewal, of hope and of happiness.

Or maybe that's what Virginia had brought when she'd barreled into his life.

A perfect early Christmas present for both of them.

* * * * *

Dear Reader,

When I wrote *Protection Detail*, the first book in the Capitol K-9 Unit continuity, I was really taken with Virginia's character. I knew she had a story that needed to be told, and I was thrilled to have the opportunity to tell it. She's been through a lot of trauma, has faced a lot of trials, but she still has faith that things will be okay. As she faces her deepest fears, she learns that the darkest of times can lead to the biggest of blessings. I hope and pray that, whatever trials you face, you know the bounty of God's love and compassion for you.

I hope you enjoyed reading Virginia and John's story! I love hearing from readers. You can reach me at shirlee@shirleemccoy.com or visit me on Facebook or Twitter.

Blessings,

Shirlee McCoy

GUARDING ABIGAIL

Lenora Worth

To Shirlee McCoy, my friend and fellow writer.
Enjoyed being here with you.

The Lord will keep you from all evil; he will keep your life.
The Lord will keep your going out and your coming in
from this time forth and forevermore.
—Psalms 121:7-8

ONE

Dylan Ralsey held open the door of the sleek SUV and waited for the petite redheaded woman who wore all black, her eyes shielded by dark sunglasses. Out of respect for her grief, he didn't speak but he did offer her a hand getting inside the big vehicle. Giving her a quick nod, he watched as she stepped up and with a practiced turn slid onto the leather seat and then abruptly removed her gloved hand from his.

Once she was inside the vehicle, he opened the back and waited for his K-9 partner, a Belgian Malinois named Tico, to hop into his kennel. After Tico did a circle and settled down, Dylan scanned the street outside the row of brownstones that sat between two stately embassies on Massachusetts Avenue in Washington, DC. All along the row, ornate wreaths decorated the private homes.

Christmas was coming.

Hard to see when you were on a funeral detail. Even worse for the woman he'd been assigned to protect. Abigail Wheaton had lost her father, a popular diplomat at a foreign embassy, to a terrorist attack overseas that had blown up the car carrying him, along with two other vehicles. In all, five people had died.

And now Washington was on high alert.

Both ahead and behind the motorcade, Dylan saw official vehicles full of Secret Service teams, FBI agents and several officers from the Metro Police, all here to help escort this one tiny woman to her father's funeral.

After confirming the all clear, Dylan finally turned to the woman he'd been assigned to protect. Pulling off his aviator shades, he said, "Ma'am, I'm truly sorry for your loss."

"Thank you." The woman looked ahead, her upswept curls glistening burnished and rich in the faint light that penetrated the darkened windows. Whipping off her shades, she sent Dylan a green-eyed gaze. "I'm not your ma'am. Please call me Abigail."

"Of course." Dylan watched the driver, a Secret Service special agent, to make sure all systems were go, and tried to recover from the flare of aloofness in her gaze. "I'll be with you twenty-four-seven for the unforeseeable future, so call me Dylan."

"For how long?" she asked as if she didn't understand.

Dylan had to make sure she did understand. "You mean, how long will we be together?" *Besides every day, all day?*

She slanted her head in irritation. "How long will I have to put up with you?"

"For as long as you need me," Dylan replied, determined to make her see the risk. "We've had enough threats against you to determine that you're in imminent danger. And until we pinpoint who's threatening you, I'll be your shadow."

"I've always had threats against me," she countered, a deep sadness darkening her exotic green eyes. "It comes with the territory."

"This is a new territory," Dylan said. He did not need a difficult subject. His job wasn't easy on a good day but when he factored in an uncooperative subject, well, that amped up the danger even more. "Considering how your father died, we need to take every threat seriously."

"I understand and I appreciate the protection." She lowered her head and cut him with another questioning glance. "But don't you have a life? People to be with during the holidays?"

"This *is* my life," Dylan said. A true statement. He was single and dedicated and because he was recovering from a gunshot wound he'd received last summer, he'd actually been glad to be assigned to help someone in need. Tico had been just as eager. They were both tired of hanging out on desk detail and going through their required paces on the K-9 practice yard.

Other than assisting fellow officer John Forrester a couple of weeks ago during a shoot-out with a stalker who was harassing John's neighbor Virginia Johnson, Dylan and Tico had been on light duty.

Two bachelors stuck in a rut. He prayed he could get back into the swing of things by being in charge of this protection detail.

Now, at least, they had some action going. But if all went as planned, this should be a quiet, easy assignment. Easy on the eye, anyway. She was a very attractive woman.

"I don't think I need that much protection," she said, her voice husky. "My father was truly a diplomat but he was used to receiving threats. He never met a stranger and he was loved by people the world over."

"But…he died at the hands of people who don't care how much he was loved by anyone. People who hate all Americans."

She turned toward Dylan with a cold glance. "You don't have to remind me of how my father died, Officer

Ralsey. I'm well aware since I've seen the horrific details in all the papers and on every channel of the evening news."

Dylan cleared his throat and remembered this woman was grieving. "I'm sorry. He was a good man."

Her expression softened. "Yes, he was. And you'll have to forgive me for taking out my grief on you. I know you're doing your job."

She put her sunglasses back on and looked straight ahead. "My father believed in the notion of world peace. He tried to look at all sides of an issue."

Dylan checked the road ahead. "They say the true measure of a man is how many friends he has at the end of his life."

"He lived for his work, sometimes putting duty ahead of everything else in his life." She took off her sunglasses again and gave Dylan another forest green appraisal. "Something you might want to consider."

Not sure what she was really trying to say, Dylan didn't take the bait. "I'm here to protect *you*," he said. "That's all I have to consider right now."

Surprise colored her face in a blush. Slamming the shades back on, she tugged her stylish black wool coat close and adjusted the cream-colored scarf draped around her neck. A full minute of silence followed while Dylan let her have her space.

He'd been briefed about Abigail Wheaton.

The only daughter of widowed diplomat Simon Wheaton, she'd moved through exotic, worldly circles and attended the finest private schools in the world. A globetrotter who also liked her privacy, she'd studied business at Oxford University and now served on the boards of many philanthropic organizations and wrote a weekly blog on the plight of refugees and homelessness, both in the United States and other countries.

Some of her opinionated posts had garnered threats. Death threats. While most of her followers supported her causes, there were always those from the fringe element who might try to do her harm. And the rising sleeper cell that claimed responsibility for her father's death was one of those groups.

She might want to ignore that in the midst of her grief and pain, but Dylan intended to keep her safe.

Whether she liked it or not.

Abigail's gaze moved over the crowd of dignitaries surrounding her father's graveside. He had told her many times he wanted to be buried here beside her mother, on the land that they both loved.

All of the Wheatons, beginning with those who had served in the Revolutionary War and those who'd served in the Civil War, were buried here. This vast country in Virginia had always been home to her father's people.

While Abigail had spent most of her life away from Virginia. She'd been blessed with an education that came from traveling the world, but she'd longed to come back here one day. But not this way, not with having to watch her father's remains being lowered into the dirt.

And certainly not with so many of Washington's elite standing somber and silent behind her. Nor had she ever imagined she'd have to be escorted around by a brooding K-9 officer and his adorable furry partner, because of the way her father had died. Or possibly because of *her* firm belief in justice for all human beings.

Her father had been murdered, plain and simple. Taken too soon, no matter the why and how.

I always thought we had lots of time, Dad.

Abigail studied the ornate flag-draped casket, her eyes burning with the need to sob. The bitter December wind sang a mournful wail that only matched the one trapped inside her heart like a captured scream. A chill covered the fields and valleys, a hint of snow in the clouds off in the distance. The sun refused to shine, its face hidden behind a gray, overcast sky.

Would she ever be warm again?

A twenty-one-gun salute. The sad, poignant sound of the lone bugler playing taps. Her father had been a soldier before he became a diplomat. And he'd been a father, first and foremost.

Now he was gone and all she had left was a folded flag in his honor, handed to her in silence by a uniformed officer.

It was too much. Abigail stood when the service was over, wobbly on her feet as the minister prayed. She'd added her own prayer to that of the minister.

Dear Lord, give me strength. Don't let me fall. Don't let me fail.

This place was too desolate in its beauty, too silent in its grief. She wasn't ready to give her father back to the land he'd loved all of his life, the land he'd missed more and more with each passing year.

Abigail loved this land, too. But not like this. Not like this. This was too heavy of a price to pay.

Dear Lord, give me strength. Give me courage. Give me hope.

She was going to lose it if they didn't get her out of here. She turned after the prayer, searching for Officer Ralsey. Like a newborn puppy, she'd latched on to him, but her attachment was more covert and sneaky than that of a happy puppy. In spite of her need to remain aloof and distant, traits the tabloids loved to showcase in her, she felt exposed and open and raw, and up until now she'd refused to let it show, refused to give the photographers being held back by yellow tape and too many police officers any satisfaction.

Officer Ralsey had changed her tough stance. He'd made her feel safe, even when she'd been rude to him.

Safe and warm.

She wanted to be warm again.

So she turned to the right and saw him standing off to the side, underneath a centuries-old live oak, his heavy overcoat hiding a multitude of weapons. The dog he'd called Tico stood with him, both of them alert and attentive, solid and sure.

Look at me. She willed the officer with the dark eyes and the inky brown-black spiked hair to notice her, to see her fear, to sense her need to have what her Southern mother would have called a regular hissy fit. *See me here, please. Help me get out of here with a little bit of dignity.*

And then, he did look up at her. He started running straight toward Abigail, his gun raised. She held the folded flag and heard the shatter of the silence in the one word he called out.

"Attack."

The dog went into action, barking and snarling and leaping into the air. At first, Abigail was sure the huge animal was going to eat her alive. But the dog sailed right past her, parting the crowd. Women screamed. Men jumped out of the way. Secret Service agents and police officers went running.

And then Dylan Ralsey grabbed her and shoved her down into the brittle, winter-dry grass and slammed his body over hers, his hands covering her head while he shielded her.

From a gunshot.

Abigail heard another shot and saw the big dog holding on to a man a few feet away from the mourners. The man screamed in pain and tried to get away but the dog held even tighter, his angry growl echoing out over the screams and shouts. Then the man went slack, his eyes wide open to the sky.

But the dog held on until Dylan shouted "Release."

Abigail gasped and tried to absorb what had happened, her heartbeat still scurrying in a state of shock.

"I've got you," Dylan said into her ear. "It's okay. I've got you." And then he held her there away from all of the chaos that had broken out beyond the solid wall of his touch.

TWO

"We need to get her out of here. Now."

Dylan shut the door of the SUV and turned to do yet another visual sweep of the hillside cemetery. Flowers were scattered like colorful handkerchiefs all around the grave site. Upturned chairs lay broken and discarded near the green tent that still stood over Simon Wheaton's casket. The spot where hundreds of mourners had been standing a few minutes ago was now empty except for the police officers and Secret Service and FBI agents who paraded back and forth like ants, gathering evidence and discussing the details with the witnesses now clustered several yards away from the scene. They'd already taken the shooter away. He'd never talk but his body could give them some clues.

"Let's go," Dylan called out the SUV window again, gathering the detail team.

"Stop!"

He whipped around to find Abigail with her hand on the door handle as if she were about to jump out of the vehicle.

The driver glanced at Dylan for permission.

She slapped a hand on the back of the seat in front of her and glared at the man through the rearview mirror. "Don't look at him. *I* said stop."

Dylan held up a hand to the driver. "It's okay." Then he turned to Abigail. "We need to get you away from here."

She shook her head, tears streaming down her face. "The flag. I—"

Dylan glanced over and saw the flag she'd been holding lying still folded on the ground near where he'd tackled her. "I'll be right back," he told the driver.

He hurried, sprinting up the hill to retrieve the tightly folded flag. Picking it up, he brushed the grass and dirt off it and made sure it was still tucked within itself.

Then he walked back to the SUV, holding the flag to his chest. Once he was inside, he nodded to the driver and then turned to Abigail. "Here you go."

She took the flag with both hands, tears still moving down her face. Rubbing her hand over the crisp fabric, she said, "Thank you."

Dylan didn't know what to say. He much preferred her stoic aloofness to this. Tears. They always got to him. But her tears, so long held at bay, made him want to hold her tight and tell her again that everything would be okay. Her tears *really* did him in. He couldn't go soft, though. He had to stay one step ahead of her tears.

Because he couldn't guarantee her that everything would be okay and he knew that from firsthand experience. She needed a good cry. She'd been through a lot in the past few days. He decided the best thing he could do right now was to get her back to the house that sat about a mile from the cemetery.

For now.

The old farmhouse had held up well, considering it had been around hundreds of years in one form or another. According to the reports and history he'd read, the Wheaton family had owned this land for centuries, and the house sitting up on a high hill had been rebuilt, added on to, rearranged and modernized through the years. A virtual maze of long hallways and mixed-up rooms.

It was a nice house but it wasn't safe. He'd done a sweep immediately after he'd been assigned to her case. Once the team had arrived here to guard her and escort her, he'd done another sweep. Too many doors and windows and stairways, too many passages and hallways. Too open and vulnerable, with wraparound porches and a big, sloping yard.

She had a staff of four people here, too. Her bulldog of an assistant, CiCi Janus, came to mind. About as approachable as a rabid raccoon, but competent and all business. Then there was the chef, the gardener and an older woman who apparently ran the house only when the Wheatons were in residence.

The chef, Louis Salsbury, was robust, bald and in his midfifties. He was married and ran a successful catering business but he helped out when guests were there. Abigail had him brought in to help Mrs. Sutton make soups and sandwiches for the many law enforcement people roaming around.

Poppy Sutton was the estate manager who looked after the place year-round as needed. She only stayed on-site when one of the family members was home. She'd fussed over Abigail like a mother hen when they'd first arrived, but for the most part, she stayed in her apartment off the kitchen.

The gardener, Sam Culliver, lived off-site but took care of the grounds year-round. He sometimes hired helpers but not during the winter months.

Then there was Orson D. Benison, the prominent and ultrawealthy lawyer who'd been a constant by Abigail's side since she'd returned home. Benison had counseled her on every aspect of how to handle her father's death, since he took care of most of Simon Wheaton's affairs and investments.

A pillar of the beltway elite, Benison had insisted on coming back to the house with them to make sure Abigail was okay.

They'd all been vetted and cleared but Dylan knew there were lots of ways around a background check. Which was why he didn't want to keep Abigail there.

He'd get her back to the farm for now, to give her a few minutes of quiet and space away from the reporters and gawkers, and then he'd take her back to the brownstone in the city. Meantime, he'd study the full report that Fiona Fargo, the team's perky whiz kid of a lab tech, had emailed him on the identity of the man who'd pulled out a gun and tried to kill Abigail while she stood at her father's grave.

After calling the head of the Capitol K-9 Unit, Captain Gavin McCord, to report in on the status of the situation, Dylan chanced a glance back over at Abigail. Her silent tears glistened in the late morning sunshine but she'd spent all her grief for now. She still held the flag in her lap, one hand brushing over it.

He dug through his coat pocket and found a clean handkerchief. "Here," he said on a gentle note. "Take this."

She sniffed and lifted her dark shades, her eyelashes still dewy with a mist of moisture. "You're kind of old-school, aren't you?"

The husky question hung in the air between them like her teardrops hung against her skin.

"My mom taught me to always carry a clean handkerchief," he explained. "She gave me a boxed set one Christmas and told me since I work protection detail I'd probably see a lot of hurting people. She was right. She gives me a new set every year now."

"Did you talk to him?"

"He's not happy. He wants this guy off the street. He has a name. Some guy the Johnson woman used to visit in prison."

"Virginia?"

"No. The lady who used to own the home. Laurel? Morris said she spent a lot of time doing prison ministry. Interestingly enough, none of her friends knew about it. She didn't participate with her church group's prison ministry. She went with another church."

"Who was she visiting?"

"Guy named Luke Miller. He was put away when he was eighteen. Spent fourteen years in prison on grand theft charges. Got out two months ago."

"Any connection between him and Laurel?"

"Aside from the fact that Laurel helped him get his education? I don't know. Morris was digging for information, but he was coming up empty. I got the feeling he's going to keep digging even though he'll be out on medical leave for a while."

"What room is he in?"

"349."

"How about Virginia?" he asked.

"She left half an hour ago. The DC police escorted her to the house. They want to walk her through. Make sure nothing is missing."

He didn't like the sound of that. When they finished, would they leave her there alone? He wanted to visit with Morris, see how he was doing, pick his brain a little if he was up to it, but his first priority was making sure that Virginia was safe.

"They did that before. Nothing was gone. This guy has another agenda."

"What?"

"When I figure that out, I'll let you know." He walked into the hall, took a couple of steps, then realized he had no transportation.

He turned; Chase leaned against the doorjamb, waiting.

"Need a ride?" he asked with a smirk.

"I need answers more, but I'll take the ride if you're offering."

"You know I am," Chase responded. "Come on. Let's get out of here."

"One night," she repeated, her green eyes flashing like dark waves on water. "One night to relive a lifetime of memories. I highly doubt I'll get it together in one night, Officer Ralsey."

Dylan tried to focus but her soft, undemanding voice seemed to mesmerize him into thinking she might be right. "I know this is hard," he said, since they could both agree on that. "I need to keep you safe."

She lifted her defiant chin. "And I'm glad you're here. I'm thankful that you...protected me this morning." She lowered her head again. "I'm grateful that you and the other officers on your team are so willing to look after me. My father would be impressed, too." She glanced around the winter-dry yard. "He and General Meyer were good friends."

"Like your father, the general has many friends," Dylan said. His boss, White House special in-house security chief General Margaret Meyer, had a lot of pull within Washington circles. She believed in the Capitol K-9 team and supported them in all their investigations. She'd expect him to do his best to protect Abigail Wheaton.

Abigail gave him one of her direct stares. "Are we going to sit here playing chicken or are you going to escort me into my home?"

"You win for now," he said. "But we're heading to town first thing tomorrow morning."

She didn't agree but she didn't argue either.

Dylan had a feeling this tug-of-war wasn't over, however.

He knew stubborn.

Because he was stubborn himself.

There was a fine line between being stubborn and

being reckless and he knew where to draw that line. Or at least he had before he'd met the enticing Abigail Wheaton.

This woman would probably test his mettle over and over.

When he came around the vehicle to help her out, she tried to hand back his handkerchief.

"Keep it," he said with a grin.

"At least I know what to give you for Christmas," she retorted, her tone gaining strength.

She dropped his handkerchief into her purse and clung to the folded flag as he and the other escorts guided her toward the rambling farmhouse.

While Dylan scanned the distant trees and hills and prayed he wouldn't regret letting her stay here tonight.

Abigail stood in her private sitting room, her gaze moving over the antique furnishings and the family portraits hanging over the old fireplace. After her mother had died when she was still in her teens, her dad told Abigail he wanted to redo her wing of the big, rambling house.

You're almost grown now, Abigail. I thought you might like a bigger bedroom and your own little den. I know how you females like closet space and lots of nooks and crannies.

He hired a designer and let Abigail pick out all the colors. Her father had always known how to cheer her up, no matter how brokenhearted she might be.

She'd redone this set of rooms twice since then and now her suite was all soft blues and rich wood, a little bit of modern mixed in with a lot of tradition. White accessories accented the blue, making Abigail feel as if she were floating on clouds.

A spacious bathroom and a deep closet accompanied the bedroom. Outside the double doors of that room,

sitting room next to the fireplace begged her to find a good book and make herself a cup of tea. She'd do that once she'd settled in for the night.

But it was past noon now and she should try to take a nap. Only she was still too wound up and in shock from this turn of events that held her captive in her own home.

Her dear, sweet, kind father was dead.

Abigail went to the fire someone had made earlier and held her hands out, seeking warmth. Why did she feel so cold?

She stared up at the picture of her parents she kept on the mantel, no matter how many times she changed the decor of this room. Their wedding picture, so many years ago. They'd been young and in love and ready to take on the world. Her parents both had a heart for service.

"I tried to follow you on that path," she said now. "I know you're up there together now because you both fought the good fight."

And yet, she held a gut-wrenching bitterness inside her heart because her father had died such a horrible death.

The images she'd seen on television stayed in her mind, greedily erasing all the good she wanted to remember.

"I hope they punish the people who did this, Dad."

A knock at her door caused Abigail to whirl, her fingers brushing at burning tears.

When she opened the door, she found Dylan Ralsey standing there with Tico. He held up a tray. "CiCi and Mrs. Sutton thought you might like some hot tea. You didn't eat much lunch, so Mrs. Sutton and Louis put together some tea cakes and a couple of little sandwiches to go with it."

Abigail waved him in. "That was considerate. I could

have come to the kitchen. Poppy—Mrs. Sutton—likes to spoil me, I'm afraid. They all do."

"You need your privacy," he said, setting the silver tray on the coffee table in front of the fireplace.

He glanced around the room much in the same way he'd done earlier when he refused to let her enter any room, especially this one, without him clearing it first. "Cozy," he said.

He headed back toward the door but the big dog sat staring up at Abigail. "Aren't you forgetting something?" she asked Dylan.

"I don't think so," he said, his dark eyes too deep and rich to tell any secrets.

"Your partner?" She pointed toward Tico.

"Oh, he's staying here with you."

Surprised, Abigail glanced down at the big animal. "I see." Then she turned to Dylan. "Has there been another threat? Is that why *you* brought my tea?"

He didn't confirm or deny that question. "Tico goes wherever you go. Until I say differently."

Then he turned, walked out of the room and shut the door behind him.

THREE

Abigail rushed after him, the dog right on her heels.

"Wait," she said, calling to Dylan. She tried to step out of the room, but the dog managed to block the door. When she shot the animal a daring glance that suggested he move out of her way, Tico returned her look with his own daring doggie-eyed stare.

"I've been tag-teamed," she mumbled while she watched Dylan hurrying back toward her.

He stopped outside the door. "Yes, ma'am?"

"I'd like to talk to you," Abigail said, wondering why she suddenly felt the need to have a chat with the K-9 officer. And wishing he'd stop being so polite.

Dylan moved back into the room and looked around, Tico matching him step per step. "Is something wrong?"

Abigail motioned him to the chair across from the couch. "No, nothing. I don't like to take tea alone." She shrugged and felt foolish because she always *preferred* to take tea alone. But not today. "Would you like to stay for a few minutes?"

He brushed a hand over his hair before stepping inside the room. "Oh, do you want some company?"

"Do you mind?" She didn't want company so much as she wanted to ask him questions regarding the information he might have on these threats that were holding her hostage with an unnamed dread. Abigail wasn't used to being told what she could and couldn't do.

"No, not at all." He checked the door for propriety's sake, left it open and sat down in the dainty velvet-covered white side chair. "Is there anything else I can do for you?"

"No." She poured herself some tea from the pot on the tray. "Would you like a cup? I can call CiCi to bring an extra mug."

"I don't…uh…drink tea," he admitted, his expression of distaste almost comical.

"Coffee then?"

"I'm fine." His gaze bounced around like a lost tennis ball. "Nice place. Your home is beautiful."

Abigail nodded. "Sandwich?"

His smile escaped before he could hide it. "If you want to call that a sandwich." But he leaned forward and took one of the trim strips of dark pumpernickel bread filled with cream cheese and black cherry jam. "I am hungry."

"Poppy and Louie will feed everyone something more substantial than sandwiches for dinner. She's an excellent cook so they sometimes butt heads. But they are both so devoted to my—to me."

"Has this particular staff been with your family long?"

He should know. Abigail felt sure he'd had anyone here vetted and researched, including her. "Since I was a young girl. Poppy came right after my mother passed away and she hired Louie and Sam later."

He finally relaxed back in the chair, his dark eyes centered on Abigail. "Are you holding up okay?"

Abigail stirred lemon and honey into the china cup full of her favorite green tea. "It's hard to answer that question. I'm fine but I'm so angry. My father didn't have to die this way. He served this country with pride and diplomacy. I…I wanted to ask you if you have any leads on the terrorist group that claimed responsibility for this."

Dylan sat up, his whole expression turning cautious and stoic. "I can't discuss that with you."

"For my own protection?"

"That and…well…we have to be careful." He put a finger to his lip, a gesture that made Abigail's heart twist inside her chest.

She glanced around, suddenly feeling vulnerable. "Even here?"

"Especially here," he replied. "This house has sat empty for months now, so we don't know what kind of activity could have gone on here while it was closed down."

Abigail set down her cup and saucer. "But your team did a sweep when I returned here, correct?"

He nodded, one hand touching his chin. "We're trying to do a sweep every couple of hours."

"Even now?"

"Until we know you're safe."

Abigail realized she'd placed him in a sticky situation by demanding to stay here instead of in the city. "I'm sorry, Officer Ralsey. I should have cooperated better."

"Dylan," he reminded her. "We'll make sure you're safe, no matter where you land." He rubbed a hand against the patina of the chair arm. "It's part of life these days. We think we know who caused that explosion and car wreck but…it's better if you don't have any of that information. The less you know, the better we can protect you."

She smiled at that. "Rather than chastise me for my inconsiderate demands, you'll work harder at your job."

"That's what I'm supposed to do," he said.

He looked so big and out of place sitting in the Louis XIV library chair that Abigail wondered why she'd asked him to stay. Dylan wouldn't divulge anything he knew. That was part of his job, too. He studied the windows and then finally got up to stare out at the tree-laden back garden.

"Is there something wrong?" Abigail asked, worried about being here for the first time since they'd arrived back at the house. Would the last ounce of her resolve and fortitude be driven away by irrational fears?

"Just checking." He walked from one paned window to the next. "We have guards patrolling the perimeters of this place but it's hard to cover the woods beyond the tree line."

"We don't have many close neighbors," she said, watching him with a fascination that took her mind off her grief and her concerns for a while. "There's another farmstead about ten miles to the east but whoever lives there tends to keep to themselves."

"Yes, we've checked out all the neighbors, distant or otherwise, but it's hard to cover every angle."

"I can understand that," she said, studying him while he wasn't watching her.

Dylan Ralsey was a handsome man. Stern and quiet with dark eyes and hair and an olive-skinned tan that spoke more of his possible heritage than of his hours in the sun. She wondered what his story was but knew now wasn't the time to ask about that.

He was here because of her. To protect her from some unknown faction. She'd do well to focus on that and not how he made her feel. She was overreacting from the stress of losing her father and traveling halfway around the world to attend his funeral. Jet lag and grief. That had to be it.

"That's what worries me," he said after her comment

about not having neighbors nearby. "You're way too iso-
lated out here."

Abigail could tell that his duty was weighing heavily
on his mind. "We can leave first thing tomorrow."

"I plan on that," he said in a tone that didn't allow for
protest. Then he turned, his suit coat open and his tie
loosened. "I'd better let you get some rest."

Did he want to be away from her that much? Or did
he feel the need to check and recheck this house and
grounds? Probably both. She obviously made Officer
Ralsey uncomfortable.

"Of course." She stood and brushed at her dress. "I
might take a nap and then I have some calls to make.
Orson Benison, my father's attorney, is advising me on
what to do next. But I insist on sharing dinner in the
kitchen with you and your men."

"That's your choice. Make sure you let one of us come
to escort you across the house." He stopped. "And jot
down anyone you call so we have a record."

He went back to the window that faced the pond and
the woods beyond it, apparently taking one more glance
outside before the sun went down. The dog, ever watch-
ful, stayed by Abigail and kept his eyes on her while
his partner blocked the sun with an imposing silhouette.

Abigail waited, her mind twirling with questions. "Is
it okay if I go online to check on my blog?"

"No." He didn't turn but he held up a hand, his index
finger pointing in the air. Tico sensed something was up
and stood. "No phone calls except to your lawyer and no
computer. You could be tracked."

"I guess it's an old-fashioned hardback book then,"
she replied, trying to lighten the mood.

He didn't respond. Instead, he grabbed the curtain
and then pulled out his phone. The dog followed his ac-

tions, alert to this man's every mood. "A flash, out behind the east edge of the pond. Could be one of ours but
send someone to check it out."

Then he turned back to Abigail. "I think I'll sit here
with you a little while longer, if you don't mind."

Abigail held a breath and pushed at the fear threatening her. "No, not at all. I'd feel better if you did."

He stayed by the window, watching. "And I'll feel better once we get you back into a more populated area."

Abigail had to admit, so would she.

Because as scared as she might be of who could be in
those woods, she was even more afraid of this man and
how he made her feel. Dylan Ralsey brought out all her
feminine longings and gave her a sense of security, in
spite of everything.

And that was something she had not expected at all.

FOUR

"All clear," Dylan told her thirty minutes later. "We checked the woods but no sign of anyone. We'll keep a patrol near the tree line." He closed the drapes. "Keep the curtains shut, okay?"

Abigail nodded. He'd told her to stay away from the windows and to sit only in the chair by the fireplace that backed against a solid wall. And that's where she'd been parked, fascinated with watching Dylan and his furry partner because she was too terrified to think about anything else. Was someone out in the trees watching her?

"Hunters move through those woods," she said, trying to rationalize her fears away. "It's that time of year."

"Makes our job tough," he retorted. "Anyone can put on an orange jacket and produce a hunting license. A good cover, but bad for us."

Abigail's guilt weighed heavy with her grief, making her tired. So tired. "So you didn't find anyone?"

"Not this time."

That implied there would be another time.

He checked his phone, checked the windows in all of the rooms and then checked on her. "I'm going to talk to the security team again but Tico will stay here with you. If he alerts and starts barking, you stay with him. Don't leave this room."

She nodded, that growing fatigue moving over her. "That won't be a problem. I think, as my mother used to say, I'm having a sinking spell. Everything is finally catching up with me. I'm exhausted."

"Nerves and grief. You need your rest," he said, pivoting around. "So I'll leave you but keep your phone nearby. And remember, don't leave this room. Tico will protect you if anyone tries to breach your suite."

"Got it." She stood to follow him to the door. "Thank you, Dylan."

His head came up when she called him by his first name, a slight surprise brightening his dark eyes. Along with a spark that practically sizzled. "You're welcome."

His gaze held hers for a second too long and then he shut the door and left the room decidedly empty. And her decidedly lonely.

Dylan hadn't told Abigail everything.

They'd found footprints. Heavy and deep. Probably hiking boots or work boots. A few snapped twigs here and there showed a path back toward a nearby stream. The dogs tracked a scent to the water and lost it. John Forrester and his German shepherd, Samson, had taken the lead, along with Elizabeth Carter and her border collie, Lady. Lady was trained to track anything that moved and she'd done her job today.

Dylan wanted to find out what was beyond that stream so they'd sent a couple of people out to search even deeper into the woods. But once they'd reached the big wire fence between Wheaton land and the next farm, they'd lost track. No footprints and no noticeable scents.

"We sent in photos of the shoeprints," John told Dylan after they'd gathered in a small den near the kitchen to assess the situation. "Might be able to identify the type of boot and narrow it down to one brand."

"That's a long shot." Dylan drank down his coffee and jotted notes on his phone app. "Could have been hunters or even paparazzi. The media is trying to get a statement from Miss Wheaton so I wouldn't put it past any reporters to at least try to get a shot of this house or her."

"The kind of shot that doesn't kill but still can do damage," Elizabeth said with her cheeky attitude intact. Her big brown eyes looked like milk chocolate. "Those tabloids make up stuff to go with the pictures."

"We have to keep at it since the graveside shooter didn't give up much in the autopsy report."

John rubbed a hand down his chin. "His background is peppered with petty crimes and work-for-hire with some definitely unscrupulous people. So far, no connection to any sleeper cells yet but we're still digging since he did have Middle Eastern ties."

Dylan figured there was a connection hidden somewhere so deep they might not ever find it. "We'll protect her from anyone who tries to get to her." He turned to John. "What *is* the latest chatter on the sleeper cell?"

John brushed a hand over his blond hair. "We're trying to connect the organization that claimed responsibility for the car explosion to a faction here in the States, but so far we don't have enough to go on since this is a brand-new threat. We've got eyes on both factions and we'll keep plugging away."

Dylan wondered if they'd ever narrow it down. "We have people over there trying to put two and two together. If we bring down the terrorist group, we can relax a little while we tie up the loose ends here in the States. But until then, we have to protect her."

John shot Elizabeth a knowing glance and then gave

Dylan one of his frosty blue-eyed stares. "You seem kind of all-in with our subject, Dylan."

Dylan kicked up out of the high-backed table chair and put his empty cup by the coffee service on a nearby console. He knew John understood. His fellow K-9 officer had gotten very close to his own subject very recently, a neighbor he'd fought to protect—and had fallen in love with. "The woman lost her father. She doesn't have any close relatives. I'm trying to be considerate. It's two weeks until Christmas. The holidays are hard... after you lose a loved one."

John gave Dylan a quiet, appraising stare. "Yeah, we've all been there." He'd lost his older brother a few years ago. Killed in the line of duty and the case had never been solved.

Dylan hadn't lost anyone to that kind of death but he'd loved someone a few years ago, back in New York, and she'd left him right before the holidays. Walked away because she couldn't handle his line of work. Because she liked Daddy's money more than she liked a police officer's salary. Either way, he hadn't dated anyone seriously since then. And he didn't plan on starting now.

An image of Abigail holding that folded flag played through his head. Dylan cleared it away and got back to business.

"I'm not sweet on anybody or anything except to find out who's harassing our subject."

No wonder he couldn't settle down with any one woman.

Some days he couldn't handle this work either, so it wasn't fair to expect anyone to cheer him on. Getting shot had sobered him, made him see that he wasn't invincible. But he still wanted to do this work, wanted to protect and serve.

"It's tough," he said, thinking of his parents who still lived back in Brooklyn in the same house where Dylan had grown up. His father had served his country and had come home in a wheelchair but Dad had never uttered a bitter word. Dylan would miss seeing them at Christmas. "Being alone is tough."

"She's alone with the whole world watching," Elizabeth said. "I can understand how you'd want to cut her some slack."

Dylan nodded. "I'm going to check on her. She was wiped out so she might be sleeping."

"If Tico needs a break, Lady and I can go sit with her," Elizabeth offered. "Girl talk soothes a lot of ailments."

Dylan smiled at that. "Might be a good idea. I doubt she has any close friends since she travels so much."

And he'd ask her about that, for sure.

He headed up the long hallway to the other side of the house, checking open doors and stepping into big, rambling rooms as he went. Abigail's assistant CiCi Janus sat in a dainty little office toward the middle of the house.

"Do you need anything, Officer?" she called as Dylan walked by.

He turned into the office. CiCi was young, solemn and efficient, dressed in the standard dark suit and white blouse. But not very friendly. Understandable that she'd want to protect Abigail since she worked closely with her on a daily basis. She'd insisted on staying here near Abigail.

Out of habit, Dylan did a quick scan of the office. "No. I'm going to check on Miss Wheaton. Have you heard anything from her since I last checked?"

The young woman shook her head, her dark brown ponytail swaying. "We had a brief meeting this morning to go over changing her schedule and moving some things around. We have a lot of work to do, but I can handle that for a few more days." She leaned up in her chair. "Mr. Benison keeps calling. He's the family lawyer and he needs to consult her regarding the reading of the will in a couple of weeks. And he reminded me of his big to-do next weekend. He'd like Abigail to attend in her father's honor, if she's up to it. It would really help if you could get her to go back into the city."

"Working on it," Dylan replied, wondering why the assistant thought it necessary to mention that since he'd been clear on how he felt about staying here. "I'll see how she's doing and I'll let her know about the lawyer. But I'm sure whatever he needs can wait for a few days, especially her making a public appearance so soon after her father's death."

CiCi got up to come around the desk, her hesitation obvious. "She's a very private person. This has been hard on her." She waved a hand toward the desk. "I'm combing through the paperwork. This is a large estate—so much to decide. But...all in good time."

Dylan held a hand on the door facing. "I couldn't agree more."

Then he headed on down the hall to Abigail's suite. Why did he get the impression that CiCi didn't want him here?

Abigail heard a soft knocking at the door.

Then she heard a woof.

Sitting up in the bed, she wiped at her eyes and tried to focus. How long had she slept?

She glanced at the clock on the bedside table. Two hours?

The dog stood and gave her an interested stare. The beautiful animal sure took his job seriously.

"Reminds me of your partner," she mumbled.

The knock came again.

"One minute," she called. She got up and tugged the velour tunic jacket over the matching soft pants and white T-shirt she'd changed into earlier, the dark gray material warm against her cold skin.

Running a hand through her hair, she headed to the sitting area in the next room, Tico following her every step.

Her heart fluttered with fear as she remembered why she was here. "Who is it?"

"Dylan. Are you all right?"

Abigail opened the door and held on to it to steady herself. But she couldn't avoid looking into Dylan's dark chocolate eyes.

He looked different now. He'd taken off his jacket and his shirtsleeves were rolled up. The shadow of a beard trekked a deliciously dangerous path over his jawline. He glanced over her, those dark eyes flaring again in that way that confused her, causing her heart to beat with an adrenaline that showed she was still alive.

The dog whimpered a greeting but stayed by her side. She smiled down at Tico, her eyes burning from crying herself to sleep. "We've had a long nap," she explained.

Dylan reached a hand toward the waiting dog and rubbed his head to acknowledge their connection. "May I come in?"

Abigail found her footing and gathered her manners. "Oh, yes. I'm sorry. I'm still so groggy. I didn't realize how exhausted I was."

He walked over to the drawn curtains. "Sun's going down. You need to eat dinner."

"Are you always this bossy?" she asked, glad to also regain some of her assertiveness.

"Yes." He turned and gave her a curt smile. "You didn't have much lunch."

"I'm not that hungry and I can decide that for myself, thank you."

He gave her a mock-stern glance and moved from window to window and then checked her bedroom before stalking back to the now-too-small sitting room. "Do you want a tray in here or would you like to stretch your legs and eat in the kitchen?"

Abigail gave that some thought. "Should I wear hiking boots since it's such a long way?"

"Touché," he retorted with a deadpan expression. "Do you want to leave this room for a while?"

She toyed with a coil of hair. "Are you *asking* me to move to the kitchen or are you *telling* me to move to the kitchen?"

He shook his head. "Are you always this difficult?"

"Yes," she replied, suddenly feeling a bit better about everything. Then she took his arm. "Let's get out of here."

Dylan grinned and commanded Tico. "Come."

They moved up the wide hallway, Tico trotting along with them. "I see someone's been decorating," Abigail said. A big Christmas tree graced the sunroom just past the bedrooms. She stopped to admire the giant blue spruce. "CiCi must have done this."

"I think I saw her moving boxes earlier, but she had the entire staff helping, too," Dylan replied. "One of our guards helped her carry some ornament boxes."

"Lots more in the attic," Abigail replied. "Nice of her to think of that, considering." She blinked back tears. "Christmas is always so special here. Poppy and Louie go all out inside while Sam makes the yard look extra special."

The lights on the big tree twinkled, blinding her to her

pain. She moved to keep going and in the next instant, one of the big windows shattered and glass spewed out into the air.

Dylan grabbed Abigail and shoved her against the wall past the windows.

Tico started barking and people came running.

While Dylan held her there and shouted orders over her head, Abigail stared at the beautiful tree that held so many family memories. And wondered if she'd be able to celebrate Christmas at all this year.

FIVE

"You okay?" Dylan's husky whisper sounded in her ear and sent shock waves down her backbone.

Abigail nodded, still holding her breath.

"One shot through the window," John called out. "We're on it."

Dylan didn't move and Abigail didn't want him to move. This man was like a human shield that protected her from every angle.

"I have to go," he finally said. Tugging her toward the middle of the house, he directed her into the office. "CiCi?"

Abigail's heart fluttered and started beating again. "CiCi," she called, fear tripping against her pulse.

Dylan let her go and gave Tico the order to guard her. "Stay in this room," he said. Then he drew his gun and hurried to the big window behind the desk.

Abigail pressed against a bookcase and watched him running his hand over the windowpanes and casings.

"CiCi? Miss Janus?" he called again as he walked around a high-backed settee on the far side of the room.

When he stopped and looked down, Abigail knew something was wrong. When his eyes locked with hers, she moved toward him, her hands going up to her mouth. "No."

Dylan held up a hand. "Stay there."

"No." She rushed to the settee. "No, I won't stay back. I have to see—"

CiCi lay dead, her blue eyes open, her ponytail wrapped against her neck like a cord. Her white blouse was stained with blood from a small, gaping hole. She'd been shot.

"Oh, no, no." Abigail felt herself falling, her legs completely collapsing underneath the weight of what she saw there.

Dylan lifted her and carried her to a nearby chair. "Hey, hey, listen to me," he said, taking both her hands in his. "I'm sorry, Abigail. Sorry." He called Tico over. "I'm going to radio this in but I'll be right outside the door, understand. Tico will make sure I hear if anyone comes near you."

She moved her head in acknowledgment but Abigail couldn't find her voice. He leaned in and placed a quick kiss on her forehead. "I'm sorry."

He was halfway to the door when she called out to him. "Dylan, how...how did this happen?"

He came back and stared down at her with a darkness that broke her heart. "I don't know yet but I promise you, I'll find out."

Abigail leaned her head against one of the big wings of the side chair, dizziness and dread tugging at her like whiteout snow. CiCi. Her sweet, efficient CiCi. Dead.

And it was all her fault.

She shouldn't have insisted they stay here at the farm.

Dylan's voice echoed out toward her, his words low and firm, his tone serious and swift while he reported in, first to 911 and then to Captain McCord. Was he planning on moving her again?

She ventured a glance over at the settee. She could
see one of CiCi's legs, her foot twisted, a black pump
slipping off her toes. A life gone too soon. Who would
do this? Who would kill an innocent young woman to
get to her?

Abigail closed her eyes and pushed at the tears that
threatened to explode in a deluge of pain and frustra-
tion. When she heard a soft woof, she opened her eyes to
find Tico right there at her side. The big dog's dark gaze
seemed to hold a world of understanding.

"You are such a sweet boy," she said, smiling in spite
of her pain, in spite of the need to crumple into a pool of
tears. "Tico, thank you for watching over me."

She leaned down and let him sniff her knuckles. Then
she reached out a tentative hand to touch his furry head.
The big dog didn't move, but his happy smile told her
he liked being petted. She'd never had many animals as
a child. Always moving around. Here where she used
to feel safe, they'd had barn cats and one mutt of a dog
named Clover who had refused to leave.

"What an amazing animal," she said to the dog she
petted now. "You are a good police officer, Tico."

Then she leaned down, her cheek brushing against his
lifted head. "What a sweet, sweet protector." With her
eyes closed and Tico's soft fur against her cheek, she sent
up a prayer for CiCi's family and for herself. She asked
God to protect her protectors, an image of Dylan and
Tico front and center on that prayer list.

When she looked up, Dylan was standing in the doorway staring at her with a dark expression that spoke of
the things neither one of them could admit.

"We found another cracked window," he said as he
advanced into the room.

"In here?" She turned toward the drawn drapes.

"Yes." He pointed up to where a skylight slanted against the gabled roof. "Up there."

Abigail stood and stared up at the dark window to the stars. "Someone came up on the roof?"

"Yes. Dogs tracked him to some trees on the back side of the house. Must have climbed up into the oak tree and followed a big limb right up to the roof. He had to have shot her from an angle, but we have a diamond-edged hole right in the middle of the skylight."

Abigail looked over at the desk. "I had that skylight installed to bring more sunshine into this room since it faces the west. Beautiful sunsets but shady and dark for most of the day. I enjoyed sitting inside the glow of that slash of light." She shook her head. "I'll have it removed when this is all over."

Dylan's sympathetic expression lasted only a couple of seconds and then he lifted her out of the chair. "I need to take you back to your suite. Officer Elizabeth Carter and her dog, Lady, will sit with you. I've got a crime scene team and my captain on the way out here. But I want to keep you away from all of this."

She nodded, too numb to react. "And what about you and Tico?"

"We're gonna have a long night," he said.

He nodded toward a waiting officer to enter the office and then he placed his palm against the middle of Abigail's back and guided her down the hallway.

When they reached the big Christmas tree, Abigail stopped. "CiCi was always so thoughtful, so considerate of my time and my work. I can't believe someone would murder her."

She touched a hand on a delicate ornament. "This isn't going to end any time soon, is it?"

"No." Dylan tugged her away from the shattered window. "I'm afraid it's just beginning."

* * *

Abigail couldn't sleep. She tossed on the bed, unable to get the image of CiCi's lifeless body out of her mind.

At around three in the morning, she got up and decided she'd try to read. When she checked the other room, she saw Lady lying on the rug by the fireplace. The beautiful border collie was different from Tico, but every bit as professional.

Lady watched as Abigail tiptoed toward the remains of the fire. Elizabeth was curled up on the couch with a throw over her but she sat up when Abigail entered the room.

"Ma'am?"

Abigail waved her back down. "I'm fine. I can't seem to settle down. And please call me Abigail."

Elizabeth sat up and ran a hand through her short dark curls. "You've had a rough few days."

Abigail nodded and then sank into the chair away from the windows. "Yes. The shock has left me numb and…frightened. Two people I cared about gone in such a short time."

Elizabeth straightened her clothes and folded her blanket.

"You don't have to keep me company," Abigail said. "I only came to get my book."

"It's okay," Elizabeth replied. "Talking can sometimes help people to remember or think about details and we need a lot of information right now. Anything you can remember."

"Ah, I see." Abigail couldn't argue with that logic. "Any word on the investigation?"

"Nothing yet," Elizabeth said. "Dylan checked in with me about an hour ago. He's in the briefing room going over things with the crime techs and the rest of the team."

Abigail let out a dry chuckle. "We have a briefing room here now?"

Elizabeth smiled. "Yes. One of the dining rooms. The interior one near the kitchen."

"Well, we have three so I'm glad someone is putting the space to good use."

"Would you like me to get you something?" Elizabeth asked.

"No, no. I'm good." Abigail got up to stoke the fire. "I'm not good but I'll be okay. I wish there *was* something I could remember that might help."

Elizabeth called Lady over and stroked her lush blond fur. "When you were overseas, did anyone approach you or try to contact you? Someone who you might feel uncomfortable with?"

"Wow, that's a loaded question," Abigail replied. "I've met hundreds of people—foreign dignitaries, soldiers, women and children who need my support, hostile dictators and hostile men who don't think I need to dabble in their business. I've been to schools and missions and palaces."

"I know it's impossible to go through that long line of people right now," Elizabeth replied, her dark eyes vivid underneath her gamine haircut. "But talking about things can help you dredge up memories and that can help us and you, too." She slanted her head. "It'll help take your mind off your grief and…well…it'll make you feel productive."

Abigail gave that some thought. Elizabeth was right. Abigail was used to taking action, to fighting the good fight for causes she supported and believed in. What better way to honor her father and to help the Capitol K-9 team bring these murderers to justice?

"Ask me some more questions," she said to Elizabeth. "I might be of some help after all."

SIX

At around dawn, Dylan went to relieve Elizabeth. She opened the door and put a finger to her lips. "Abigail finally went to sleep about an hour ago."

"Tough night," he whispered, wondering how Abigail would be in the morning. She'd had too many shocks too close together. "Go and get some rest and I'll catch you later."

Elizabeth silently alerted Lady that their shift was over. "Oh, we had a good talk earlier."

Surprised, Dylan lifted his chin. "About what?"

"Everything," Elizabeth said. "I tried to draw her out and see if she remembered anyone who might seem threatening or...creepy."

"And?"

"She thought of one man in England. A diplomat visiting from a small Middle Eastern country. She'd met him before that at her father's embassy, too." Elizabeth gave him a name and Dylan typed it into his notes. "He sent her a sympathy note two days after her father was killed and asked to speak to her as soon as possible."

"That would have been about two weeks ago then," Dylan said. "Red tape caused the funeral arrangements to be delayed."

Elizabeth nodded. "Yes, and he's also made some comments on her blog over the past couple of years. Nothing threatening but he seems to be an admirer."

Or he could be pretending to be an admirer. "Got it. So the girl talk paid off."

"In more ways than one," Elizabeth retorted with a snarky grin.

"Want to share?"

"No. Some things need to stay between us girls."

Dylan had to wonder what else Abigail had told Elizabeth. He should have known his engaging and animated colleague would be able to converse with Abigail better than he could.

But then, Elizabeth didn't have an extreme crush on the woman.

There, he'd finally admitted it. After a little over twenty-four intense hours with Abigail Wheaton, Dylan's whole perspective on dating and having a personal life had shifted off its high horse and taken a tumble down to earth.

This woman might be worth getting to know. An unbelievable revelation since he'd sworn off any kind of relationship because his work had caused his last one to crash and burn.

Or maybe it hadn't been his work. Maybe he'd loved and lost while the woman who'd walked away hadn't loved him enough. Accepting that was a revelation in itself.

Accepting that gave him the courage to try again. Getting to know Abigail made him consider his preconceived ideas.

But he had to fight against that for now.

He had a sworn duty to protect her, to keep her from

being killed inside her own home. In fact, he had decided that moving her might make things worse at this point.

And that was why he was so surprised when Abigail marched out of her bedroom fully dressed and glowing with energy.

Then she said, "I've decided you're right and we should go back to Washington, Officer Ralsey. I want to see and be seen and I want to meet with as many people as I can. My father would expect me to carry on and he'd also want me to be brave. I won't let whoever is doing this make me cower in darkness."

Dylan shook his head and ignored the floral smell of her perfume and her misguided sense of duty. "No, that is not a good idea, considering—"

"Considering that my assistant is now dead and that my father died at the hands of some sort of extremist group? I beg to differ."

"And why would you want to expose yourself that way after what you just said?"

She touched at her upswept hair and came to stand in front of him, her green eyes now blazing with purpose. "To draw out a killer, of course."

Dylan shook his head so fast, Tico swung around toward him in a spin. "That's not how this works."

"I know how things work," she retorted. Then she picked up the house phone and called for coffee for two.

Was she back in the game or pretending away her grief? She'd either try to bury all of that emotion and cause herself even more pain, or she'd spin out of control and have a meltdown. Either one could be dangerous for her.

"Listen, Abigail, I've thought things over and I don't think we can risk moving you right now."

She stopped in her pacing to stare at him. "But you said we'd go back to DC today. That this place was too vulnerable. And since I was shot at and…CiCi is now dead, I have to agree with that assessment."

He moved closer so he could look into her eyes and make her understand. "Someone is out there in those woods watching our every move. If we load you into a vehicle, they will follow us or possibly ambush us. It's too risky."

"So I'm a prisoner in my own home?"

"No. You need to stay out of sight for a while."

"Even in Washington?"

"Until we can figure out how to get you to Washington," he said.

She put her hands on her hips, the black dress she wore falling in graceful folds from her waist to her knees. "Then let's figure it out. I mentioned a diplomat to Elizabeth during our chat session in the wee hours this morning. Omar Dibianu. He seems honest and he's a decent man but…I've always felt a bit odd around him."

Dylan noted that. "Yes. She briefed me on him. I plan to do a search and see what we come up with."

"That's all well and good," Abigail said, her dainty teardrop pearl earrings dancing around the swoop of her long, side-swept auburn bangs. "But…he's attending a function this weekend at the home of my father's attorney and he expects to see me there. Mr. Benison has invited me to this soiree and…I'd like to go."

Dylan could almost see the inner workings of her beautiful brain in her forest green eyes. "I don't think—"

"Look, Mr. Dibianu knows me. He trusts me but I don't trust him. He seemed a bit too keen on asking me questions about my father's whereabouts during our visit to London a few weeks ago." She shrugged. "I don't know but I got the distinct feeling Mr. Dibianu was watching me during one of the dinners we attended."

Dylan pushed away the stab of jealousy that image solicited. He had no right to be jealous of anyone who might be interested in this woman. And he needed to stay on track here because someone watching her could mean more than a passing interest. It could mean her life.

Keep the subject safe.

At all costs.

"You don't have to attend this function so soon after all of this. Abigail, you don't need to prove anything to me or anyone in Washington. You only need to rest and let us do what we need to do to keep you safe."

She whirled, the soft smile and confident stance gone now. "Don't you understand I have to do something, help in some way, to find out who is doing this? Who killed my father? Why? Who came here to my home and managed to shoot CiCi right under my nose? It isn't right, Dylan. And I'm helpless to do anything but sit here and wait?"

He moved toward her but she turned away.

"You're not helpless," he said, wishing he could say more. "We're closing in on this new sleeper cell that's taking responsibility for the car bomb that killed your father and we're combing these woods day and night so hopefully, we'll get a break soon."

She turned back, her eyes brimming like twin pools of dark green water. "I'll make a deal with you then. We have three days before the gala Saturday night in Washington. If you haven't found any answers by then, I'll attend the gala since Mr. Benison asked if I'd be up to attending in my father's honor and because it gives me a perfect opportunity to speak with Omar Dibianu. I might be wrong about this man and his motives and I pray that I am. But I have to start somewhere."

She brushed back her long bangs. "I'll be fielding calls after word gets out that CiCi is dead. I have to be able to function without caving. I won't sit back and wait to be killed in my own home, and staying busy with a normal routine will help me to focus and be more alert."

She was right. He wanted to end this but Dylan knew more danger would be coming. He thought about everything that had happened so far. He did want to move her and get her back to a more populated area but these people might be ruthless enough to harm a mansion full of movers and shakers in order to get to her.

"What if we're putting others in danger by letting you attend this function?"

"I'll go in 'dark,' as all you gung ho people like to say. You can smuggle me in and…since it's in Washington and several politicians will be guests, I'm sure the place will be heavily guarded anyway. If we sense any danger, you can whisk me away immediately."

Dylan thought over all the worst-case scenarios and then he thought about being able to get closer to someone who might be a suspect. It could be a good lead. Or it could turn into a disaster.

"I tell you what," he finally said. "I'll have to clear this with my superiors but while we're here for the next few days, you could answer the responses on your blog, provided my techs can monitor and trace anyone who comments."

At her surprised glance, he added, "It's worth a try since we might pick up a pattern or a clue. And if we haven't made headway by Saturday, you can attend the event. Did you already RSVP?"

She nodded. "CiCi had done that on my behalf, yes.

Before…before I lost my father. He and I were going to attend together once he came home for Christmas."

Dylan moved close to her and said, "Well, don't change that plus-one."

"What do you mean?" she asked, holding her hands in front of her.

"I mean, if you go I'll be right there by your side. I'll be attending as your date that night."

SEVEN

Abigail sat staring at her laptop. Tico lay near her feet, her constant companion these days.

She was in a small sitting room near her father's wing of the house. This had been her mother's favorite room since it was in the middle of everything. Near the kitchen but close to Abigail's dad's office, too. Her mother had often taken care of her own schedule from the antique writing desk in this room while her father worked next door in his office.

Abigail remembered running back and forth between the two of them, happy and loved and so naive. Those special memories pierced her now with a bittersweet sharpness that made her catch her breath.

She was all grown up and all alone.

She couldn't bear to go into her office and even if she could, it had been cordoned off with crime scene tape.

Each time she thought about how CiCi had died, a chill went down Abigail's backbone. She needed to decide what to do about her father's things and what to do about his office…and her own. Could she ever work in there again?

She'd change this long, sunny room into a new office. Or she'd shut down this house and move somewhere else. Once this was over, of course. She would never sell this place but she didn't have to stay here. She could buy a townhouse in the city or anywhere she wanted for that matter.

But she had a lot to do before she made any rash decisions. Right now, she was going over the comments from her recent blog post. Dylan had coached her on what to say and how to handle any threatening comments.

Don't engage. Keep the conversation flowing and stay on task. If you get into an argument with anyone, they might do more than leave comments on your blog. Or they might figure out we're trying to track them.

Abigail didn't intend to argue with anyone. She'd never done that on her blog anyway.

She'd talked about losing her father and she'd thanked everyone for their condolences. Such an outpouring of love and prayers had come her way and she was truly grateful for that.

She'd gone back over some of the highlights of his life—her parents' happy marriage, their travels, his accomplishments within diplomatic circles. The Wheaton legacy had spanned centuries and now she was left to carry on that tradition.

If she could get through the next few weeks, she'd be okay. She'd find a way to continue her father's work.

Abigail stood up and wished she could open the blinds. But Dylan had been very strict in warning her to be careful. He'd also cautioned her on how to handle the blog.

No mention of how your father died or that CiCi was shot in your home. As far as the rest of the world knows, you're here in seclusion for the time being.

Seclusion. Abigail had always been an introvert with extrovert tendencies. She loved her alone time, the quiet time where she could reflect and write her posts on everything from homelessness to war to politics. But she also enjoyed being out with others, talking with people who wanted to make a difference in the lives of those less fortunate and sometimes talking to those who were suffering and in need of someone's help.

She'd listen, respond, do her research and then she'd present her opinions on her blog. Right now, she wanted to scream and lament the unfairness of losing the people she loved the most. But she was a Wheaton. She had to be strong and carry on, no matter how much her heart was breaking.

So she paced the sitting room and enjoyed the shards of stubborn morning sunbeams that tried to break into her forced imprisonment, Tico's trusting eyes following her every move.

She knew if she tried to exit this room, Tico would block the door and bark. For her protection, as Dylan always pointed out in his curt, no-nonsense way.

"At least you're a good listener," she told Tico.

Dylan had that same rare trait. He listened, his dark eyes holding hers, his very presence reassuring and calming.

The man was good at his job but he didn't indulge in idle conversation.

Abigail wished she could talk to her father. About everything and about nothing. About Dylan and how each time he entered a room, her heart did a quick bump, bump, bump that excited her and confused her.

When her computer beeped, Abigail cleared her head and went to see if she had any new comments on her blog. What she saw there sent chills all over her body.

Wicked, worthless people go around telling lies.
—Proverbs 6:12.

The Bible verse was followed by a lone comment.

You are wicked and worthless. You will pay for your sins.

Abigail sat staring at the words, a sick feeling settling in her stomach. What had she done to garner such
a harsh condemnation? Had this person killed her father
and CiCi?

She picked up her cell and texted Dylan: Odd comment.

In about a minute, she heard his footfalls on the old
hardwood hallway floor. She'd learned to listen for his
steps and that alone told her she was getting too involved
with her protector.

"What do you have?" he asked without preamble, the
intensity of his expression telling her this was serious.
Tico's ears lifted but Dylan didn't greet his partner with
the usual affection. He came around the desk.

She showed him the caustic comment.

Dylan read what was on the screen and then placed
a call on his phone. "Fiona, are you looking at Abigail
Wheaton's website blog?" He nodded. "Good. Let me
know what you find."

He ended the call and turned to Abigail. "We should
be able to find out where the comments originated from,
hopefully without too much trouble." Stopping to glance
at the screen, he added, "Well, actually that depends on
if he moves around a lot from one IP server to the next.
That would mean he goes through a maze of proxy serv-
ers and then things get real tricky. Like hunting for one
particular rat in New York City."

"Amazing," Abigail said, not sure if she was talking about modern technology or Dylan's need to track
a killer.

"This could give us a break in the case," he said, rubbing a hand down his spiky hair. "It's a start, anyway."

Abigail saw the fatigue in his eyes, but he smelled fresh and he was wearing a clean white shirt and dark trousers. He must have finally slept a little and then cleaned up.

Nicely.

"Can it be that easy?" she asked to distract herself.

"It's never easy," he replied, his gaze drifting over her like a warm wind. "We have to keep at it."

"I still want to attend the event this weekend," she said, her tone daring him to dispute that notion.

"But we got a hit on the blog," he reminded her. "That was the deal."

"The two might not be connected," she countered.

"Abigail—"

"Let's consider all of our options after you hear back," she replied, glad to be in control again.

"That's not how this works," he said, effectively taking away her small amount of control.

"I see." She paced again, turning away so he wouldn't see her utter despair. Which was silly. She should be grateful and she was and yet…she wanted to have a pity party.

"Hey." He turned her around, his dark eyes bright with sincerity. "I know how difficult this is for you, being shut up in here. But…hopefully this trace will help us." He pointed to her laptop screen. "You've got a lot of support out there and one nasty comment. That could be the one that gives us all the answers."

She shook her head. "I'm behaving like an immature ninny, but you're right. This is hard, being back here during Christmas. It's supposed to be the season of peace while we celebrate the birth of Christ. I miss the good times we had here...back when things were so special in my family."

His expression changed, softening. "This situation makes it hard to look back."

Glancing toward the closed blinds, she said, "We should always honor those special memories and hold them dear. We never know when things can change in the blink of an eye." Then she turned back to face Dylan, a resolve weighing at her shoulders and making her broken heart heavy. "I'll do whatever you decide. I want this over and these people brought to justice."

"So do I," Dylan replied, one hand stroking Tico's furry back. "I won't rest until we make that happen."

When his cell buzzed, he gave her a soft smile and hit the phone screen. "Fiona, what did you find?"

He listened, his brow furrowing, his gaze on Abigail.

Abigail started pacing again, her mind whirling with speculation. Then she glanced back at her blog and hit refresh.

Another message from a different screen name.

We're sorry for your loss and we watch with anticipation what you will do next. The screen name only showed the letters *OD* followed by an address she didn't recognize.

Dylan tapped his phone and let out a sigh. Then he walked over to see what Abigail had read.

"We've got a lot going on here," he finally said. "And you deserve to know the truth."

EIGHT

"What do you mean?"

Dylan saw the trace of fear in Abigail's eyes and wished he could wash it away. But she had a right to know that things could get worse for her.

"We think the same person is making different comments on your blog. It's called trolling. They make a comment that will disrupt things, then they make another comment bashing the comment they just made, using a different IP address. And it keeps going."

She listened and shook her head. "So one person can agree with me and then post something hateful in the next comment, using a different email or screen name?"

"Yes." He studied all of the comments she'd received over the past few hours. "Someone could send you a condolence that sounds very sincere and then a few comments later, blast you for your beliefs."

"Unbelievable."

"That's the world of cyberstalking and trolling."

"So did you find the person who made that horrible comment?"

"Not yet. Very sophisticated operation with lots of bells and whistles, things I don't even understand. But Fiona and the lab techs are studying it closely. They've managed to trace most of the comments to an overseas server."

"The mysterious sleeper cell?"

"Could be one and the same." He hoped so.

She sank down near a small fireplace and put one hand underneath her chin. "CiCi was my computer whiz. She knew all about how to navigate the internet."

Could that have been why CiCi was murdered? "Why don't you take a break for today? Our techs are putting people in place to check this out."

"What happens if you discover this person or persons' whereabouts?"

"We go in and take him or them into custody for questioning."

"And possibly connect them to my father's death?"

"That could be a probability, yes. They could be sitting somewhere in Europe at an internet café. But if that's the case, we'll get them."

She turned pale, her porcelain skin silky white. "I don't want to think about this anymore. It's horrible to imagine that kind of evil power."

Dylan took her by the hand and lifted her up. "Are you hungry?"

She looked down at their joined hands. "No."

"Why don't you try to rest?"

She pulled away and placed her arms around her midsection. "I can't really rest. I see my father's casket and I hear Tico barking. I see CiCi's body lying there and I see the blood—"

Dylan tugged her back around. "What would help?"

Her gaze shifted from tormented to tender. "It's nice of you to ask but I don't think you can bring back my father and CiCi."

No, he couldn't. But he could try to cheer her up. "I

have an idea. Why don't you go and get comfortable. Try to relax. Tico will be with you. I'll come and get you for dinner and we'll have a quiet night. We won't talk about any of this."

Surprise dotted her face. "Are you asking me on a date, Dylan?"

He grinned. "Let's pretend it's a date. I can't date you right now, Abigail, but a man can hope."

With that, he admitted how he felt and watched a pretty blush color her shimmering skin. She didn't speak at first.

Dylan wondered if he'd overstepped but she finally smiled up at him. "I'd like to visit with you and get to know you. I want to hear all about your family and your dreams and how you came to be a K-9 officer in Washington, DC."

"I'm boring," he said, relief washing through him. "I doubt we would have ever met before."

"Don't doubt," she admonished. "God sometimes has plans for us whether we see them or not. My mother used to say there are no coincidences."

"Good point." He guided her out of the office and signaled to Tico to follow. Had God brought them both to this point?

Dylan couldn't answer that nor could he explain why evil people did things to harm good people. But he could work hard to serve and protect. A small comfort for now.

Abigail whirled at the door. "My laptop."

"I'll take it with me and read over the comments again, show the others, too." he said. "You need to rest, remember?"

"All right. I am tired but I'm not used to taking naps during the day."

"Well, if you have to be cooped up inside at least you

can nap when you want. It's getting colder out. Might snow tonight."

"Snow," she said. "At Christmas. Now, that will make things better all the way around."

Dylan smiled and thought about how the snowfall could cover sounds and hide footprints but he didn't tell her that.

If she wanted snow, he'd pray toward that end. And he'd find a way to let her see the snow, too.

Dylan called in his report and discussed this newest development with Captain McCord. He also mentioned the Washington gala that Abigail wanted to attend this weekend. The captain was aware of the gathering since General Meyer would be there.

"Miss Wheaton seems determined to go, sir."

"Well, she's not exactly a prisoner. We can't make her stay secluded and Mr. Benison is a close family friend and her father's attorney. If she feels a need to get out and see people, our job is to protect her no matter what she wants to do."

"It might be good to get her out of the house but…we can't expose her to any more danger."

"That gala will probably be one of the safest places in Washington," McCord said. "High security since a lot of movers and shakers will be attending. The president won't be there since he's in Europe but the vice-president is attending. It's your call, Ralsey."

"Thank you, sir. If she does connect with Dibianu there, we can make sure before she goes that he's been thoroughly vetted. He has to be cleared before he sets foot on the grounds of that estate, anyway."

"Yes, but he still might have a hidden agenda."

"I'll talk to her again and plan accordingly," Dylan replied.

He ended the call, then responded to texts from his fellow team members, Elizabeth Carter and John Forrester, checking in. He texted back his appreciation, then sat staring at the dining room table. He'd asked the chef to prepare Abigail's favorite meal. Dylan had to be careful with this. He'd worked protection detail for a lot of people in the past few years. But never anyone compared to Abigail. She was like cut glass, delicate but strong all at the same time, with a shimmering essence that gave her a beautiful dignity and grace.

Whoa. What was he thinking?

You can't go there.

Abigail had come from a life of privilege and power. She could move through circles he never wanted to be a part of.

You're an average Joe from Brooklyn, he reminded himself. *Blue collar meets lacy collar. It won't work.*

It hadn't worked the first time he'd fallen in love. He couldn't forget that no matter how erratic his feelings for Abigail seemed right now.

"You sure are lost in thought."

Dylan glanced up from staring at Abigail's laptop to find John Forrester staring at him from the doorway.

"Just thinking," he admitted. "I'm reading back over the comments. We have a list of all the email addresses but it's like sifting through flour to get through the maze of proxies some of the comments are coming from."

John lifted away from the door. "We've interviewed the remaining staff members regarding their whereabouts when Miss Janus was killed. Chef Louie, as he likes to be called, was at a Christmas party with his wife. Lots of people can vouch for him. The gardener says he was at home sound asleep. His wife confirmed that. And Poppy Sutton only remembers getting up to get some water around eight or so. After that, she put on her white noise and went to sleep."

Dylan nodded. "I don't think she'd be capable of climbing up on the roof to take someone down with a silenced gunshot."

John smiled. "No, but she does brag about being an avid deer hunter."

Dylan made a note of that. "Hmm. Which means she must know a lot of the local hunters. We might need to ask her about that angle."

John pulled out a chair and checked his watch. "Samson is with some of the other dogs going through his paces before the storm hits. I'll need to get back to him but, Dylan, do you suspect locals on this?"

"I suspect everyone on this," he replied. He glanced out at the growing dusk. "And I don't like being here at all."

"We'll keep a good watch," John said. "I hear you're treating Abigail to dinner?"

He pulled a blank face. "She needs to eat a good meal. Chef Louie and Mrs. Sutton worked for hours making pot roast and baked rolls. And some kind of fancy dessert."

"I think it's called Apple Brown Betty," John replied, his expression as blank as Dylan's. "And of course, she can't eat alone, right?"

He finally grinned, feeling sheepish. "Okay, you got me. I want some pot roast and some of that apple stuff."

"Yeah, that's it. You're in it for the food."

"You better believe it. I'm a bachelor, after all."

"Not for long, friend." John got up with a cheeky grin and headed for the door. Then he turned and got serious. "Be careful, Dylan. I'm not one to judge since I fell hard for Virginia about five minutes after I met her, but you're dealing with something that could be broad-reaching. Watch your back."

"Always."

He watched John leave and then he glanced out at the coming night. He figured John hadn't only been warning him about the danger out there. His friend was warning him to guard his heart, too. "Always."

NINE

Abigail woke up and glanced at the clock.

6:00 p.m. She'd fallen asleep curled on the couch in her sitting room and dozed for close to a half hour or so. She sat up and watched bemused as Tico did the same.

"Dinner?" Abigail asked, thinking she would miss Tico when this was over. She'd also miss Tico's human partner.

She got up and went to wash her face, her thoughts a constant mixture of despair and determination. In the past few days, she'd fallen asleep every night with tears streaming down her cheeks. She missed her father with an open-wound ache and now she mourned poor CiCi with a heart already weighed down by grief. She'd made a call to CiCi's family but Dylan had suggested she not watch the news or read anything online since this whole turn of events was probably the lead item on all the news shows and political blogs.

After she'd changed into jeans, boots and a long cardigan sweater, Abigail realized she was actually nervous about this dinner. But why? Why should she be nervous around Dylan? Sure he was handsome, competent, demanding and interesting. But...she should stay in her room, alone with her tears and her worries.

Fear not, for I am with you always.

That verse calmed Abigail and reminded her that no matter what, she'd find a way to hold steady. And she'd certainly find a way to get through this enticing dinner.

She hoped. Her cell buzzed and thinking it was Dylan, she smiled. But her whole system stilled when she read the text.

Urgent. I need to see you. Perhaps at the Benison event this weekend? Omar.

Why would Omar Dibianu send her a text?

When a knock came at her door, Tico and she both hurried to make sure it was Dylan. After hearing his deep voice, Abigail opened the door and gave him a shaky smile. She was pretty sure Tico was doing the same. "Right on time."

He offered her his arm. "Your meal is ready." He seemed different, more relaxed.

"What is it?" she asked, needing to know. "I can tell you're not quite as somber and brooding as you usually are."

He stopped her by the door to her suite, a wry smile moving across his face. "I have good news. Based on our foreign intel, a team made a raid in an obscure little village and arrested several people in this so-called sleeper cell. Abigail, I think we've got them."

Abigail put a hand to her mouth. "Oh, that is good news." But it was a bittersweet victory. "It won't bring them back, but...Dylan." She reached up and hugged him. "Thank you so much." She stood back. "Is it really over?"

"We need to make them give up their faction here, but I hope so," he said, his dark eyes holding hers. "And... I'm suddenly starving."

"I smell something wonderful," she said, amazed. Tucking her phone in her pocket, she decided she'd tell him about the text from Omar as soon as they'd eaten. At least now, she might not have to question Omar's motives. "Is that Poppy's Yankee Pot Roast?"

"She says it's your favorite."

"It is. It was my father's favorite, too."

"I'm sorry." He stopped before they came to the open spot where the window had been shot out. "I didn't consider that."

"It's all right," Abigail said, the cryptic text still on her mind. "In fact, it's perfect. Father would approve completely."

Dylan's features relaxed again. "Good. Because it smells wonderful and I'm pretty sure the whole gang will want sandwiches later."

"We are feeding them, too, right?"

He nodded. "Are you kidding? I think I'd be run out of here on a rail if I didn't offer them some of this dinner, especially since we got positive news."

Abigail wondered if they'd all be at dinner with Dylan and her but she refrained from asking since that would sound too obvious. "Glad to hear that. Poppy always makes way too much for two people."

Her heart did that little skip of regret and grief. She longed for her father to be sitting at the table, waiting for her. But...Dylan was here and she was glad to have him. She noticed how he blocked her from the windows when they moved past the lone Christmas tree. And how he shielded her when they reached the closed door to her office.

Dylan was not only a good officer. He was kind and considerate, too.

They made it to the main dining room, where someone had placed poinsettias and blooming amaryllis plants along with a glittering gold reindeer figurine on the antique buffet and placed the good Christmas china out on the long table.

"I see Poppy and Louie have continued in the Christmas tradition," she said, touched beyond words. "This is so lovely."

"I think it was a combined effort," Dylan said. "Lots of elves hanging out around here."

She laughed at that. "I'm picturing you with big ears and an elf hat on your head."

"That ain't gonna happen," he quipped before pulling out her chair. "Consider this as part of our own Operation Santa Claus Mission."

Abigail sat down and enjoyed the warmth of his smile along with the beauty gracing this room. "I haven't been feeling very festive but this helps a lot."

Dylan sat down and served up the sliced roast, complete with potatoes and carrots. "This looks great."

"And Poppy's yeast rolls, too." Abigail thought she might actually weep with joy. But it would be a joy tinged with pain. "Thank you for doing this," she said to Dylan. "I didn't think I'd ever have an appetite again but I'm actually hungry."

"Well, let's say grace and dig in," he replied with a boyish expression.

She let him speak and he gave a short but spiritual prayer, asking God to protect them and others in danger.

Soon they were quietly eating. Conversation flowed but with a somber low-voiced discussion that highlighted the grief shrouding the house.

Abigail leaned back after eating most of the food on her plate. "I know we aren't supposed to discuss… things…but I'm concerned about CiCi's parents. I called and gave them my condolences. I should probably release a statement, too."

Dylan put down his knife and fork. "We'll do that first thing tomorrow. General Meyer informed CiCi's parents about this positive news and explained how we had to keep you under wraps right now. Our department did release a statement announcing we'd captured most of the members of the sleeper cell and that we're doing everything we can to find out who else might be behind this."

She nodded and watched as the twinkling lights on the buffet sparkled against the chandelier's hanging crystals. Then they went back to personal talk and soon Abigail had put Omar's text out of her mind. Dylan told her about his family up in Brooklyn.

"So you're a native New Yorker?"

"Born and raised there. I try to get back when I can."

"But this year, you can't because you're here protecting me."

His dark eyes held hers with a determined warmth. "I've had worse assignments."

Ignoring the way those soft-spoken words charmed her, Abigail said, "What has been your worst assignment?"

He took a sip of coffee and pushed away his plate. "Well, I got shot in the shoulder this past summer. Almost got blown up that same night. My buddy John Forrester dragged me away from the explosion. Then he and I were involved in another explosion a week or so ago. House caught on fire but neither of us was injured, thankfully."

Abigail's heart seemed to stop beating. "You could have been killed. I might not have ever known you."

That was almost too much to bear, considering how he'd saved her twice now. "You must promise me you'll be careful. I couldn't take it if anything happened to you or anyone on your team."

"We know the risks," he said. "Part of the job."

"I'm not sure I could deal with that kind of risk on a daily basis," she retorted, grief coloring her words. "How do your loved ones get through each day?"

The crestfallen look on his face caused her to pause. "I'm sorry, Dylan. Right now, I'm overly sensitive to anyone being put in danger."

"It's okay," he said. "Let's talk about something else."

But the mood changed after that. Abigail didn't know what to say or do but she'd obviously hit a nerve with him. Had he lost someone he loved due to his job?

"I have an idea," she finally said. "Why don't we let the others come in and eat? I'll serve dessert."

He nodded and stood. "Good idea. We don't want this food to go to waste."

"No, we don't."

Abigail wished she'd been more considerate. Dylan took his work very seriously and he'd probably sacrificed many relationships in order to do his duty.

And he had to avoid having one with her for that very reason. Just as well since they'd only met a few days ago and she had a lot of grief to work through before she even began to think about falling for someone. Not to mention staying alive.

And yet…she watched as he texted his team members, his expression edged with a frown.

"They'll be in soon," he said. "But before they come in, I have a surprise for you."

"You do?"

He came around and took her by the hand. "Let's go into your mom's office—where we were earlier."

"Oh, all right. And after this, I need to tell you something." She followed him and Tico up the hallway and took the turn toward the back of the house.

"Don't turn on the lights," he said.

She noticed the blinds were open. "What's going on?"

"Wait and see."

He tugged her inside. "I need you to sit on the floor right next to the couch."

"I have no idea what you're doing but I suppose it's some sort of covert operation."

"Very covert."

He helped her down and then he and Tico plopped down with her. "Now," he said. "Wait for it."

Again, he texted someone.

And then he took her hand, causing Abigail to yet again be intrigued and baffled.

"Now," he said, his words a soft whisper.

Abigail watched out the window. And then, a tree out toward the back of the property came to life with all sorts of colorful lights that twinkled and blinked in the night.

"Oh, my." She gasped and held her hands to her face. "Oh, Dylan. Oh, this is…beautiful."

"We're all doing our jobs but we took turns stringing lights to celebrate tonight. That and patrolling the perimeters, of course. We can't stop that until we have the all clear."

Abigail had never seen a more beautiful sight. "It's amazing. So lovely. So thoughtful. I don't know what to say."

Before she could change her mind, she leaned over and gave him a quick kiss on the cheek. "I'll never forget this."

Dylan grabbed her hand and held it for the briefest time, his gaze moving over her face. Then he let her hand go and they sat there for a few minutes.

"Time for dessert," he said. "But as long as we're here, I'll bring you in here every night and make sure you get to see this tree all lit up."

Abigail went with him back to the dining room, and soon the room was filled with canine officers and their furry companions. They took turns checking on the outer patrols and making sure her property was safe but for a while, they talked and laughed and entertained Abigail until she felt sleepy and content.

Dylan sent Tico into her suite and made sure she was safe. "I'll be taking couch duty tonight," he said. "Tico will be with you."

Abigail nodded and wondered what it would be like if they could have a date that didn't involve his sweeping the room for intruders. She also wondered what it might be like to give him a real kiss instead of a feathering of her lips against his skin.

But would Dylan ever be willing to consider that?

TEN

"It's snowing."

Abigail heard the words from one of the officers and almost rushed outside to see what everyone was talking about. But Dylan's hand on her arm steered her back down in her chair.

They had returned to the dining room and since it was in the middle of the house away from windows, it had been deemed the best place for Abigail to visit with everyone.

"I'll take you to our secret place again to see it," he said, his husky words fluttering against her hair.

She nodded and thanked God again for all of these amazing officers and their K-9 partners. When this was over she fully intended to give a big donation to the Capitol K-9 Unit.

"The Apple Brown Betty was so good," Dylan said, trying to cheer her up. "I'll have to sweet-talk Mrs. Sutton into giving me that recipe so my mom can make it."

"Poppy guards her recipes with an ironfisted spoon," Abigail replied with a laugh. "But I'll see what I can do to put in a good word for you. She's hard to impress but I'm thinking she'll like you a lot."

Dylan grinned at that. From outside they heard laughter and dogs barking. "The kids are having fun out there," he said, referring to the team.

"Snowball fights," she said, wishing she could have some fresh air. "They've worked hard so I think they've earned a good time."

Dylan must have sensed her restlessness. "Let's go get you a coat," he said. Then he pulled her up and together they hurried to her suite.

Abigail came running out into the hallway, Tico on her heels. She'd grabbed a huge brown parka with a hood. "Is this okay?"

Dylan nodded. "We'll only be out there for a couple of minutes. I've got guards posted but I can't promise you that something won't happen."

"I'll be careful," she said, glee filling her heart.

He took her to the back door where everyone stood watching the snow. "It's coming down pretty hard."

"I can't wait to feel it on my face," she replied, her heart lifting for the first time in days.

He turned to adjust her hood, his eyes meeting hers, his face inches from her. "Abigail…"

"I know," she said. "I know and I understand. You have to remain impassive and professional. And you don't want to fall for anyone like me again, right?"

He leaned so close, she thought he might kiss her. "It's a long story. I'll tell you later."

Then he pulled her out into the night air and her breath caught while she lifted her head to the sparkling white flakes falling from the sky.

Dylan did a visual of the nearby woods and held Abigail close to the shrubbery, hoping he'd obscured her from any rifle scopes but he also felt a sense of relief that this might be over soon. The others did the same while they pretended to be playing in the snow.

John Forrester came up beside Dylan and Abigail. "We all need to get back to work so enjoy a couple more minutes."

Dylan lifted his chin in acknowledgment. "Understood. I appreciate the effort."

John grinned. "Are you kidding? We needed a break, too. No offense, Miss Wheaton."

Abigail turned in her fur-trimmed hoodie. "This is so wonderful and I'm so thankful. But I don't want to put any of you in harm's way if it's still not safe. I can go back inside."

John shook his head. "We've done a search throughout the woods on all sides of your property. Nothing for now. Not even a lone orange-vested hunter."

Dylan didn't want to complain but he glanced out into the shadows beyond the yard. "It's been quiet today. Almost too quiet. Word must be out so they're scurrying away."

"Don't jinx it," John replied. "I've got to get the others back on task." He glanced from Dylan to Abigail and back to Dylan, then nodded, and again, Dylan knew his friend understood that something special was developing between him and *his* subject. Things had worked out well for John and Virginia, but still, Dylan had a job to do. He had to stay professional until he was absolutely sure of things.

In a matter of minutes, the other officers were gone, dispersed to make rounds, two to a team, around the house and grounds. Which left Dylan standing here behind the shrubbery, watching the snow gather on the grass, with a woman who smelled like spring.

He wanted to take Abigail into his arms so he could pull his hands through all that dark red hair and kiss her right here in the snow. But he couldn't do that.

She turned, her hood falling away, snowflakes melting

against her bangs. "Dylan, you went to a lot of trouble to make me feel better tonight." She lifted one hand in the air. "Even bringing in snow."

He chuckled. "I think a higher power covered that but it does add to the festive mood of the night."

Her eyes brightened, a rich green that looked like a lost forest against the dark sky. Then she reached up her hand and touched his jaw, her fingers whispering over his skin like a promised kiss.

Dylan didn't think. He pulled her into his arms and kissed her, his fingers crushed against the silky threads of her hair. She put her arms on his shoulders and leaned into the kiss while he shielded her from the darkness of the woods.

For those few moments, the world was safe and warm and full of the peace of Christmas.

And then a gunshot pierced through the woods and echoed out over the fallen snow.

Dylan lifted Abigail and pushed her back toward the door behind them, Tico barking at his heels. Once they were inside, he hurried her away from the door and windows.

"Stay here," he told her before ordering Tico to stay with her. Then he rushed back toward where they'd come from, shouting into his earwig.

Abigail should be used to this by now, but how could anyone get used to being under siege day and night? She'd been in Dylan's arms, kissing him! What if he'd taken a bullet for her?

Thinking about what he'd told her—that he'd been shot this past summer—she closed her eyes and wished she hadn't been so impulsive. She'd wanted him to kiss her and he had, because she'd pulled him close, giving him an open invitation.

Because she had thought they were finally safe.

But whoever was out there watching took that distraction as a perfect time to try to kill her. If they ventured out beyond those tall shrubs…

Then she remembered the text. She'd kept stalling on telling Dylan about it. Now she'd have to let him know about Omar's plea.

She couldn't think of that now. She had to catch her breath and try to gather herself. She wouldn't cave in to the fears clawing at her soul. She wouldn't cower in fear. Dylan's strength gave her a new kind of courage.

The kind that came forth when you realized you'd fight to the end to save the ones you loved.

At two in the morning, everyone gathered in the less formal dining room to assess what had happened.

"We followed the scent up to the main road," Elizabeth said, her dark gamine bangs spiked against her forehead like twigs of broken wood. "Vehicle tracks off the shoulder, lots of mud and shoe prints but nothing we can use. The snow covered a lot of it."

"We'll go back over it in the morning," John suggested. "And we'll search for shell casings near that stand of tree to the west."

Dylan nodded and glanced around at the now somber group. "I'm sorry I brought her out of the house."

"We went over everything and agreed," John reminded him. "You kept her in the shadows, Dylan." He shifted on his seat and took a long swig of coffee. "Look, these people are pretty good at evading us and we thought we had them—or at least that capturing the others would send them into a retreat. They seem to know the layout of this place and they're obviously watching every move we make. You're doing the best you can, considering."

Considering that he'd breached protocol and kissed the woman he was supposed to be protecting. No one said that but Dylan could almost feel the condemnation in the air.

"It won't happen again," he said. "We have to get her out of here and I think the best thing we can do at this point is take her back to the city and let her attend that gala. We might stir something up and finally be able to figure out who's coming after her." He studied his notes. "I'll call the captain and go back over this with him. Meantime, he might have more information on the people they brought in today."

"And we've still got Fiona and her crew searching for anyone else flagged from the blog comments," Elizabeth reminded him.

Dylan nodded. "How can these people be so relentless without us nabbing at least one of them?"

"They walk around among us," John replied. "You know how that works. My brother worked hard to track this kind of group and got himself killed."

"Well, don't let that happen to you," Elizabeth said to him. "Virginia wouldn't like that."

John smiled at her words. Dylan was glad his friend had found someone to spend his life with and Virginia Johnson was a quirky, nice, loving woman. He'd regret it the rest of his life if something happened to John.

Or any of them, for that matter.

"I'm changing my tactics," he said. "Gotta get my head back in the game. I won't let any of you down."

"We know that," Elizabeth said, giving him a high five. "But you might want to convey it to…her."

They all looked toward the hallway leading to Abigail's room.

"I think she already knows," Dylan replied.

ELEVEN

Abigail woke to waves of sunshine breaking through the closed drapery in her bedroom. She rolled over and saw Tico lying by her bed. The big dog gave her a doleful stare but didn't make a move.

He wouldn't until she stood, she knew.

They'd placed an armed guard by her door now, too.

And Dylan and Elizabeth had taken turns on the couch in the other room.

She closed her eyes and remembered that kiss. A moment of pure bliss in the middle of so much darkness. A warmth that flowed like a glowing light right through her heart.

And then, that shattering that brought night birds out of the trees and scared the forest animals.

Someone was still out there trying to kill again.

She got up and rubbed Tico's fur; then she took a quick shower and put on warm sweatpants and a matching hoodie, all done in a deep gray to match her mood.

When a knock sounded on the door, she expected to find Dylan standing there. But it was Poppy.

"Poppy, come in," Abigail said, surprised since Poppy Sutton rarely left her room by the kitchen. "I see you brought coffee."

"And toast," Poppy said, her almost white hair clipped and pressed to her head as if she'd ironed it. "You need to eat better, Abigail. You're way too thin."

"I'm fine," Abigail said, motioning to the table in the sitting room. "Please, sit and tell me how you're holding up with all this excitement around here. I hope you're planning on going to visit your family for Christmas."

Poppy wore a white sweater and a black skirt, her sensible loafers polished and shining. Her wide glasses gave her the look of a wise owl. "It's horrible. We're all afraid for our lives so yes, I fully intend to head to Richmond next week—if that's okay with you."

"I'm so sorry," Abigail said, getting up to roam around the room. "I'm planning to send you all away. It's too dangerous."

The older woman looked affronted. "We won't leave you here by yourself but we do all have plans. You need to find better people to protect you. What do these city people know of our backwoods? People can hide in these hills for months on end."

Confused, Abigail whirled to stare at Poppy. "Do you think someone has been living in the woods?"

"No, no. Of course not." Poppy got up to leave. "I worry about hunters being shot or children getting caught in the crossfire. We've never had any trouble here and... you owe it to your father to keep it that way."

Abigail tamped down the anger brewing in her tired system. She knew Poppy meant well, but sometimes they had different views on things. "I owe it to my father to *stop* this. CiCi is dead because someone out there is after me. My father died because someone wanted him killed."

"But why would they want to hurt you, honey?"

"I don't know," Abigail admitted. "I truly don't know."

Poppy tugged Abigail close. "I don't want anything bad to happen to you."

"I'll be fine," Abigail said, tears burning at her eyes. Blinking, she stared at Poppy's filigree necklace. "I'll be okay. I've decided to go back to the city anyway. I'm going to a big event that was already scheduled. I think my father would want me to keep up appearances on his behalf."

Poppy's lips pursed in agreement. "He always was a stickler for showing grace under pressure."

"Yes, he sure was," Abigail said. "All the more reason to honor him by finding his killers."

Then she turned and walked back into her bedroom. "Leave the tray, Poppy. I'm not very hungry right now."

But she was determined. She wouldn't put her staff here in the path of these evil, unrelenting people. Dylan had been right all along. She'd be safer in the city.

Later that day, Dylan found Abigail in the sitting room where he'd taken her to see the Christmas tree they'd all worked to put together for her. Had that really only been yesterday?

He'd been up most of the night, the memory of their kiss giving him the stamina to keep moving. But he came to a stop when he saw her there at her mother's desk, writing thank-you notes to the people who'd sent flowers and food and sympathy cards since her father's death.

She wore comfortable clothes, soft velvety blue sweats and a cute sweater jacket. Boots that covered her tight-legged pants. Tico alerted—traitor. And Abigail looked up and into Dylan's eyes.

"There you are," she said, getting up. "I need to talk to you."

"I know." He figured she'd been avoiding him for a reason. "I need to talk to you, too. About last night."

Disappointment and regret flashed through her eyes but she lifted her chin. "Any word?"

He rubbed his eyes. "No. We found the usual. Footprints too murky to identify and vehicle tracks off the side of the main road. Abigail, listen—"

"I want to go back to Washington," she said before he could explain. "I'm putting my staff in danger, too. It's not right and I've been selfish by trying to hang on to the last shreds of joy by staying here for Christmas."

"Washington?" He'd come to talk to her about that. Dylan advanced in the room and gave Tico a "good boy" pat for hanging with Abigail all day. "So you still want to go through with this."

"Yes. I need to make a statement to the press and handle some other things. We still have time to get there before the big gala at Orson's house. I need to be there, for my father's sake and to possibly flush out anyone who might be involved."

"That's why I came to talk to you," he said, weariness shooting through his system. "I agree with you."

"You do?" She sounded surprised.

"I talked it over with Captain McCord and he cleared it with General Meyer. She'll be at the event, too, and she has assured me you'll be well protected. But we all agreed that this Dibianu fellow needs to be considered. So far, his background is clean. He's been a loyal diplomat for years and seems to have a solid reputation but we need to see what he's up to regarding you." Placing his hands on his hips, he said, "Don't approach him. Let him seek you out. I'll be with you and you can introduce me as a friend who worked with your father."

She nodded. "Okay. So...what's next then?"

"We get you packed but we'll leave tonight. One vehicle a few hours ahead of us. We want to leave a few official-looking vehicles here to throw anyone off." He watched her pacing and wondered if they'd made the right decision. "Promise me you won't do anything to put yourself in any danger."

"You mean, don't do anything stupid, right?"

"Not stupid, but courageous, daring, determined—"

"You do know a little bit about how my mind works."

"Yes, and that scares me. A lot."

"I think you're scared of things that have nothing to do with someone trying to kill me."

She had him there. "You're right, but that's for another time."

She glanced down and then back into his eyes. "Dylan, before we go I need to tell you that I got a text right before dinner last night. From Omar Dibianu. In all the excitement, I didn't get a chance to show it to you but I haven't responded yet."

Dylan put his hand out, palm up. "Let me see it now."

Had she forgotten or was she deliberately withholding things from him? He read the text and then turned to her. "Abigail, this is too dangerous."

"Or too important to pass up," she countered. "What better place to meet him? We'll be surrounded by so many Secret Service and FBI people and your team, too, nothing can happen to me. He might have information on my father's death that can substantiate what you've found."

Dylan didn't like it but if she insisted on this rendezvous, he'd be standing right there with her. "Let me analyze this and get back to you. And, Abigail, next time alert me immediately."

"Okay." She gave him a glimpse full of resolve and

finally came to stand in front of him. "Now that we've agreed on that, what should we do about that kiss?"

Dylan wasn't sure how to answer that but he was sure that he wanted to kiss her again. Their kiss had been amazing, touching, perfect. But he had to get back to business, especially with the developments of the past few hours.

"What do you think we should do about it?" he asked.

She placed her hands together in front of her. "I should apologize to you since I forced the issue. I wanted to kiss you so...I did. It was wrong of me, but...it's been a long week."

While Dylan was glad to hear she'd wanted to kiss him, it couldn't happen again. "Look, Abigail, you didn't do anything that I haven't thought of doing all week."

Hope colored her eyes but her expression showed a lot of doubt. "So you admit you're attracted to me?"

"It doesn't matter how I feel. I overstepped the boundaries and broke protocol. Things got out of hand. I can't protect you if I'm distracted and you can't be distracted from showing me important communications that might endanger you. From now on I have to remain impassive and maintain a professional distance from you."

The hurt in her eyes tore at him like ice crystals against his skin. "I see," she said before she turned away. "I understand. And since I don't want anyone else to get killed on my behalf, I'll leave you alone."

He reached up and snagged her arm to pull her back. "I'm sorry but *you* could have been shot last night."

"But I wasn't," she said, "because you blocked me. You could have been shot, and that's something I can't imagine. I wish I hadn't been so pathetic that you took me outside to calm me down."

His ebony eyes registered disapproval. "You're not pathetic. You're grieving and you're still in a state of shock."

She shook her head. "I don't want to endanger anyone, certainly not you."

"That's my job and that's for me to worry about."

"Yes, and you've made it very clear that your job doesn't allow for personal relationships. Especially since I was so horrified about what you have to deal with on a day-to-day basis. So…I get it, Dylan. You don't have room in your life for emotional complications."

Dylan didn't want to hurt her but right now, his first priority was to protect her. She'd get over that kiss and she'd forget about him once she was safe again. He'd never forget her and he'd never forget their kiss.

But he needed her to understand one thing. "I can't go down that road again, Abigail."

She gave him a disheartened stare. "You mean that road where someone broke your heart and caused you to become so stoic and unyielding. You're assuming that I'll be like the woman who obviously caused you a great deal of pain, but…you might be surprised to find I'm made of stronger stock than that."

"I wouldn't be surprised by anything about you," he said, turning to leave. "And yet, you surprise me on a daily basis."

He stopped at the door. "We'll leave at full dark."

"I'll be ready," she said, her back to him. "And I'll be so well behaved you'll hardly know I'm there."

Oh, he doubted that. The awareness between them fairly danced off the walls. He stood there at the door for a full minute, caught between the need to kiss her again and the need to keep her alive. When she waved a hand at him in dismissal, he finally turned and walked away without another word.

Because really, there wasn't anything left to say.

TWELVE

Abigail's nerves jingled like tiny bells with each mile they took that brought them closer to the city.

She stared out the window as they headed away from the farm and toward the road to I-95. Now that they were headed back to Washington, DC, she wondered how she'd handle the crush of well-meaning people who'd want to hug her and give her more condolences at the gala. But her nervousness didn't come so much from seeing people again as it did from trying to avoid Dylan's solemn black-eyed stare.

He'd secreted her away in one of Poppy's coats and hats, in an unmarked car that looked so bland no one would notice it zooming along the freeway. Tico had gone on ahead with the others but Dylan was right here by her side.

And she couldn't face him. Humiliated and hurt, she tried to understand what kind of life he must lead, doing this day after day. No wonder he didn't want anyone special in his life. While his work scared her for more reasons than being in danger, she admired him and respected him enough to know he was right about them. She couldn't force him to take notice of her when he was working so hard to save her. And she still had enough dignity and decorum left to step away, so she went back to her aloof self and tried to gather her strength for the upcoming weekend.

Work had to come first in his profession. And it always would. He'd made that clear. Well, finding a killer was high on her priority list, too, so she hoped she'd be the bait to bring that killer out. A risk she had to take.

But really, Dylan had a point.

Could she live like this every day? Could she allow someone she cared about to go out there over and over to put himself in harm's way?

They'd been tossed together in a heightened stare of awareness and she had to consider that this would all be over soon and he'd be gone. She still had to get her father's affairs in order and decide what to do with herself next anyway.

They weren't meant to be together.

Right now, he was so near she could reach out a hand and touch him. So she kept her tricky hands clutched together in her lap and watched for the first sight of the Washington Monument.

"Hey," he said after a few moments of silence, leaning over toward her where they sat in the backseat. "How you doing?"

Was he able to feel her thoughts? "I'm fine, thank you."

"You're the perfect subject," he said with a chuckle. But she sensed a nervous edge to his laugh.

"How's that?" She didn't look at him, couldn't look at him for fear he'd see the truth in her eyes.

"You've been very considerate and accommodating, spoiling all of us. So thank you."

"I have my moments."

He let out a grunt, followed by a sigh. "Actually, that's not true. You're not the perfect subject. In fact, you've given me concerns from the moment I first saw you."

Finally, she whipped around and shot him what she hoped was an authoritative glare. "So you've pointed out with your oh-so-mixed messages."

"I am confused about you, but I have to let that go for now. I'm trying so hard to resist you, Abigail. But it's not easy. I need you to understand that."

She wouldn't let him see the hope in her eyes. "I understand that you've been hurt by a woman, Dylan. And I understand that because of what she did, you can't find happiness again." She edged toward her corner of the seat. "But it's okay, really. I'll be back to my full schedule soon and I'll travel a lot and possibly follow in my father's footsteps so it's silly for me to think about…a relationship with anyone either."

"Especially someone like me, right?"

She wouldn't hurt him by making a pointed comment. "I don't know," she said, "since I don't really know you all that well. This week hasn't been the best way to get to know someone, has it? I wish we could have met under different circumstances."

They were approaching the city now and headed toward the discreet neighborhood near Embassy Row where they'd taken her the day of the funeral. The lights glowed around the Jefferson Memorial off in the distance. She saw Dylan's silhouette etched in shadows, saw the way his eyes stayed on her.

He scrubbed a hand down his face and then reached out his index finger and traced it over her wrist. "If the circumstances had been different, we probably wouldn't have met at all."

Then he pulled away and started directing the driver on where to park so they could get her safely out of the car and inside the house.

And probably, so he could get her safely away from his heart.

THIRTEEN

Dylan let out a long breath the next day and escorted Abigail into the Capitol K-9 headquarters building. "Good job on the press conference," he said, his hand on the small of her back. They'd announced the capture of several members of the Middle Eastern group and mentioned they were still tracking members in the United States. Then Abigail had spoken briefly.

"Thank you."

She looked every bit the ambassador's daughter in a dark navy suit with a skirt that skimmed her pretty legs and discreet matching heels that only highlighted her curvy calves.

And he needed to peel his eyes back to front and center.

But she smelled good, too. Like a fresh garden in the middle of winter.

Keep your nose in the air.

Dylan did a quick scan of the nearby buildings. So far, so good. This place was like a fortress so he felt pretty secure bringing her here for the press conference. General Meyer had attended in a show of support and she and Captain McCord had stood on each side of Abigail along with the ever-present Orson Benison, while she thanked everyone for their thoughts and prayers and talked about her assistant CiCi and her father, ending with the assurance that soon these killers would be brought to justice.

"You were a pro," he said once they had her in a conference room with Tico by her feet.

"Part of *my* job," she quipped, her attitude back to the calm, cool redhead he'd first met a week ago. But he could see the fire burning underneath that controlled demeanor.

A fire that tempted him and scared him.

He didn't want her to turn reckless on him.

"Okay," he said, bending down to rub Tico's thick fur, "you stay here while I handle a few things. Then we'll get you back to the safe house so you can get ready for tonight." Then he stared up at her. "*Are* you ready for tonight?"

"As ready as I'll ever be." She crossed her legs and sat back. "Go and do your thing. I have my buddy here." Her slender hand slinked down to Tico, her knuckles offered so the dog could sniff her skin.

And get a whiff of that great-smelling perfume.

Back in the game, Ralsey.

He stood and nodded. "I'll send someone in with some water and I think we have some coffee and crackers around here. Some Christmas cookies."

"What, no donuts?"

"Ha, ha."

He reluctantly left her there with some magazines while he reported in and went over the plan for tonight. He'd be with her at all times and they'd have officers planted throughout the crowd. They'd also coordinated with the locals, the Secret Service, the FBI and CIA. This event would have almost as many law enforcement people here as invited guests.

Dylan wanted to get it over with.

* * *

She wanted this over with and done.

She wanted one more hug from her father and one more long talk with him late at night.

She wanted CiCi here fussing over her and reminding her of where she needed to be next.

She wanted Dylan to open up to her and let her help him heal. He might do the same for her. Christmas was a time to look forward. A new year, a new beginning, but holding steady with the traditions of the season. And the reason for her faith. The love and sacrifice of Christ, that could overcome even the worst in life.

Abigail closed her eyes and prayed for guidance and peace and once again asked God to keep Dylan and his team safe. She'd tried to scan the crowd at the press conference, fear and indignity merging in her mind. For a split second, she thought she'd seen Omar Dibianu there in the crowd but it must have been her imagination. She wouldn't talk herself out of trying to connect with him at the Benison affair. It was a long shot but they all needed it to work.

"It has to work so we can end this. Please, dear Lord, help us."

She felt a cold nose on her hand.

When she opened her eyes, Tico was there. He gazed up at her with unconditional devotion.

"At least you're willing to show me your heart," she whispered to the faithful dog. Then she rubbed his back and cooed at him, pouring all of her emotions into thanking at least this one good officer for protecting her.

Dylan listened to the latest briefing, concern and fatigue pulling at his system. They'd had a hard time tracing a couple of the IP addresses from Abigail's blog but

FOURTEEN

The big white mansion shined like a jewel in a neighbor‑
hood near DuPont Circle, and tonight one of Washing‑
ton's finest historical homes was all decked out for the
holiday season. But the decorations were subtle and un‑
derstated. An evergreen wreath trimmed in red ribbon
hung on each of the impressive floor‑to‑ceiling windows
in all levels of the home and two huge matching wreaths
graced the beveled glass doors. Candelabras stood lit with
white candles on each side of the entryway and a huge
tree that could be seen through the lower level window
offered a welcoming sight.

Abigail had been here before many times so she knew
the history of the Benison Mansion. Orson D. Benison
owned a thriving law firm that had been in his family for
generations and while he'd inherited most of his wealth,
he'd accumulated even more through solid investments
and buying into a couple of internet start‑up companies.
He had helped her father with his investments, too.

He also controlled politicians on both sides of the aisle
and represented the crooked ones who were willing to pay
a hefty sum to use his services. Her father had not partic‑
ularly cared for Mr. Benison's boastful attitude but he'd
always accepted invitations to events here as a courtesy.

Fiona said she'd crack them sooner or later. But the techs
had picked up a pattern that was disturbing.

Omar Dibianu followed Abigail's blog and lurked on
almost a daily basis on her website. Now he'd become
more bold, sending her that text in such an urgent man‑
ner. Could he be part of the faction behind these attempts
on her life?

"What if we're taking her right into a trap?" he asked
the captain after they'd established that they didn't have
any other solid leads.

"The man would be foolish to try anything tonight,"
Captain McCord replied. "We've swept the venue every
hour on the hour and we'll keep doing that right up to
and during the event. We'll have eyes on everyone en‑
tering and leaving the place and you'll have eyes on our
subject. At best, we'll be able to corner the man and ask
him a few questions."

"And the worst?" Dylan asked, knowing the answer.

"The worst is that an attempt is made and we get
her out of there and capture her assailant all in one fell
swoop."

"I don't like it," Dylan admitted. "I shouldn't have let
her talk me into this."

"She wanted to come and we all made sure it was her
decision." The captain glanced at his watch. "You need
to go get all fancied up. Be aware and be careful, got it?"

"Got it," Dylan replied. He'd be on hyperalert the
whole night.

Four hours later, Abigail stood in front of a full‑length
mirror, wearing a royal blue empire‑style dress with sheer
capped sleeves and a sheer bodice embroidered with tiny
white pearls and crystals. CiCi had helped her pick it out
at a very upscale shop in Paris weeks ago.

Her assistant had sent her holiday clothes to the farm, knowing Abigail would eventually go back there.

The festive dress and her mother's diamond stud earrings should cheer Abigail but she only felt defeated and gloomy. Her father had always looked dashing and gentlemanly in a tuxedo.

Dabbing at her eyes, she had a moment of panic. Maybe going to this big event so soon after her father's death was a bad idea. But she'd made the decision and she'd stick to it. Get in, make the connection and get out.

That was Dylan's motto. He'd told her they'd go in and mingle, let her connect with the very anxious Mr. Omar Dibianu and see what he had to offer and then they'd get her out of there.

"You can do this," she whispered to her reflection. "You have on a good concealer, after all."

Her mother used to say a good concealer underneath the eyes could hide a multitude of problems.

I need more than a concealer, Mother. I need you and Daddy back.

Abigail touched a hand to the shimmering bodice of her dress. She knew her parents were in her heart so that gave her the courage and comfort she needed to make this one bold move.

When a knock came at her door at precisely seven o'clock, she knew it had to be Dylan. The man was very punctual.

"How do I look?" she whispered to Tico. The big dog gave her an approving doggy smile.

She took a calming breath, checked herself in the mirror and asked who was there.

"Dylan," he said.

Abigail opened the door and lost her heart.

Dylan in a tuxedo, his black hair glistening and curl-

ing around his forehead and ears, his eyes inky a[nd] open. And on her.

He did a thorough sweep, taking in her dress[...] his gaze came back to her face. "Are...are you r[...]"

She nodded, unable to speak, unable to move[...]

"You'll need a wrap."

She whirled to get her white wool evening cl[...] her matching clutch. When she turned around, Dy[...] there. He took the wrap and put it over her shoul[...] hands lingering near her neck.

"You look amazing," he said, his breath war[...] ear.

Abigail closed her eyes and willed herself t[o...] aloof and unaffected. But oh, she was affected. [...] shaken and moved and changed and...she was f[...] a man who didn't want someone like her in h[...] man who had decided he couldn't afford to ha[...] one to love.

"Abigail..."

For a brief moment, she felt as if he need[...] something more, something personal and inti[...] he held her, his hands warm on her skin.

"Let's go," he said, shifting away.

Abigail turned and nodded, regaining he[...] "This should be an interesting evening."

He gave her one of those silky black Dyl[...] his hand touching her elbow. "You can say th[...]"

and so he could keep abreast of the beltway undercurrent. And because he admired this historical home and enjoyed the impromptu tours Mr. Benison conducted for anyone who might be interested.

Now, as the black limo they'd borrowed to allow them to merge with the crowd slowly made its way up the driveway, Dylan reached across and squeezed her hand. "Remember, don't do anything dangerous."

Abigail kept her surprise to herself. He'd hardly said a word to her on the short ride over but she'd turned to find him glancing at her several times. They'd gone around the block twice to throw off anyone who might be following them and he'd checked and rechecked ahead of them and behind them. But his fingers wrapped around hers now in a touch that was anything but business. The warmth from his skin scorched a message straight to her heart. Dylan meant business, in his career and in the way he took care of a woman.

Abigail had never felt so secure and safe in her life. And in that moment, she realized she could be headed for serious trouble with this man. She could so easily fall for him.

"The same to you," she quipped. "Stay safe."

He nodded and let go of her hand. "Stay there until I can come around and open the door for you."

She did as he told her, thinking he was also a gentleman, but this courtesy had more to do with scoping the cars unloading all around them and taking in the scene. Still it was nice to be pampered and guarded.

Already a crush of glamorous people moved up the wide stone steps leading to the massive wooden and glass front doors. The shrubbery surrounding the house glistened in the snow, bright white lights shining like stars against a blanket.

Some of the massive trunks of the live oaks had been strung with the same twinkling lights and giant festive balls hung from their lower branches. The whole place was tastefully decorated, making the night seem even more festive.

When they reached the first landing between the steps and the house, Dylan spoke softly into the earbud he wore to communicate with the other officers on duty tonight. "We're approaching the entryway."

Abigail glanced around and took in the mass of people who'd come to this grand party, a chill moving over her as the wind shook snow off the trees.

She had to wonder. Was a killer walking amongst them tonight?

Dylan guided Abigail through the crush of people, his hand on her arm, his gaze moving over the crowd. The sooner they located Omar Dibianu, the sooner he could get her out of here. They'd decided to let her enter through the front so the crowd could help protect her. But Dylan still worried. So he held on to her, wishing Tico could be here but the crowded environment didn't allow for dogs inside the house.

The big dog was safely waiting in his kennel in the garage, warm and taken care of until he might be needed.

Dylan prayed that time wouldn't come.

He glanced at Abigail, watching as she greeted people, her smile not so bright, her eyes still dulled by grief. She looked beautiful, ethereal, shattered. But she stopped and accepted hugs from people with sympathetic expressions or took pats on her arm from people clearly surprised to see her here tonight.

And then Benison came down the wide marble staircase and headed straight for Abigail, his tuxedo tailored to the last stitch, his smile stitched on as perfectly as the tuxedo.

Dylan got a strange feeling as he watched the debonair millionaire give Abigail a solicitous hug, but he shook Benison's hand after Abigail introduced him again.

Benison knew who he was, of course, since they'd met out at the farm right before the funeral. But the silver-haired gentleman played the part of gracious host with such ease, Dylan had to smile at the garish overkill in the big room.

"I'm so glad you came, Abigail," Benison said, his hand clasping hers. "It's an honor to have you here."

"My father always enjoyed your parties," she said, her tone low. She gave Benison a soft smile and then withdrew her hand from his.

Benison moved on to his other guests, but Abigail kept up the pleasantries for nearly an hour before she turned to Dylan with a panicked glance.

"Are you all right?" he asked before tugging her into an empty alcove near the back of the house.

"I need some air." She fanned herself, her eyes suddenly misty green. "I thought I was ready for this but I'm a bit overwhelmed by seeing so many people who knew my father."

He sat her on a bench. "I'll find you some water. Don't move."

She bobbed her head, leaned back against the wall. "I'll be okay."

But Dylan wasn't so sure about that. She looked pale, drawn and exhausted. He watched her as he stood at a nearby bar and waited for the water. They'd been here long enough. Dibianu obviously wasn't going to show.

Abigail took a deep breath to calm her nerves. Since when had she succumbed to panic attacks? She pushed at her hair and sat up, willing herself to stay still and find some sort of center.

A hand on her arm startled her and she looked around to find Omar Dibianu sitting there beside her, his dark eyes wide with concern. "Miss Wheaton, it is imperative that we speak in private. I have been trying to contact you since your father died. I need to warn you."

Warn her?

Abigail stood and searched for Dylan. He charged toward her with a glass of water, his expression grim and determined. He'd spotted Omar. "Yes, I understand," she managed. "What is this about, Mr. Dibianu?"

"Not here," the nervous man said. "Your father was trying to get home so he could talk to you about a very urgent matter. We need—"

Before he could finish the sentence, a waiter hurried up, stopped close to Dibianu and stared directly at Abigail. "Next time, you'll be the one."

Dibianu let out a gasp and fell to the floor, blood flowing from his side. Abigail screamed. Dylan dropped the glass, ran to Abigail and lifted her up into his arms and carried her down a hallway, away from the gasps of the people who'd just witnessed a murder.

"He was trying to warn me, Dylan."

Abigail kept saying that over and over as the motorcade moved through traffic slowed by a full-blown snowstorm.

Dylan held his cell phone to his ear and listened to her while he reported back. "What did he say?"

"He said my father wanted to get home and tell me about something. I don't know. He… They stabbed Omar before he could tell me." She let out a gasp. "The waiter told me I'd be next."

"That will not happen." Dylan talked into the phone and then ended the call. "Stabbed and dead. I'm sorry, Abigail."

Her mind whirled with regret. "I insisted on trying to talk to him. It's my fault."

"No, it's the fault of whoever is behind this," Dylan replied, his hand in hers. "We're going to get you back to the safe house and we'll regroup."

"What now?" she asked, thinking she might not ever be free of these threats and attacks.

"We keep fighting," Dylan said. "We'll get to the truth."

Abigail had to wonder about that.

"I'm afraid," she said to Dylan. "Not so much for myself but for everyone around me. I'm afraid for you."

"Don't worry about me," Dylan said, his hand in hers. I'll be fine, okay?"

She nodded, the lump in her throat burning with such a raw pain she couldn't speak.

So she sat silent and held on to Dylan's hand, her prayers tripping over her fears. What had her father been so concerned about?

They were a block from the safe house when Abigail heard a popping sound and then the SUV skidded in the snow and went spinning out of control. Abigail bounced and felt the vehicle turning, falling, rolling.

And then her world went dark.

FIFTEEN

Dylan woke to bright lights and people in white uniforms, a disorientation weighing him down with the same force as being pulled underwater. He tried to sit up, tried to remember what he was supposed to be doing.

Abigail!

"Sir, lie still."

A nurse, her hair short and spiky, her frown no-nonsense.

"Where am I?"

"George Washington University Hospital," she said. "You were in an accident and you've suffered a head injury and some lacerations. Please lie still."

"Abigail?" he said, trying to sit up.

The nurse turned to someone else in the room. Dylan tried to lift himself up again but he drifted back into blackness. Then he felt a hand on his arm.

Captain McCord stood by the gurney, his expression etched in fatigue. "How you doing, kid?"

Dylan shook his head, blinked. "Not so good. Where is she, sir?"

"You don't need to worry about that now."

Dylan gritted his teeth to stop the spinning in his head. "Where is she?"

"They took her, Dylan. But we're searching for her. I promise you, I'll find her."

Dylan didn't say anything. He closed his eyes and willed himself to be still. Because he couldn't let the captain know, but as soon as his head stopped spinning he intended to find Abigail himself.

Abigail jerked awake, her mind numb with shock and fear. The taste of blood left a metallic tinge of bile in her throat but when she cried out, no one came to hear her. The gag around her mouth suffocated her, but Abigail swallowed the dread and tried to focus. Her left shoulder throbbed and burned and she felt a wet, cold stickiness on her throbbing right temple. Her blue chiffon dress was torn and dirty and her hair was down around her face. The memory of being tossed and hitting her head against the door caused her to close her eyes. A wreck. The SUV had flipped.

Dylan. He'd been holding her hand.

Dylan? Was he alive? Would he find her?

She shivered from shock and cold and fear. She didn't know where she was but she took calming breaths to keep the panic at bay. She had to escape, had to find a way to get out of here.

Wherever here was.

The room was dark and musty with shadows playing across a high-beamed structure. A barn? She listened and tried to squirm free of the ropes holding her hands behind her. Did she hear voices?

Yes. And footsteps. Someone was approaching. Her heart accelerated into a cadence that matched the urgent footsteps.

A big door creaked open and a streak of light blinded her.

She twisted, trying to see, trying to search for some sort of exit.

A tall, menacing form stood in front of her.

"This should have been so easy," the familiar voice said on a low growl. "Set up the sleeper cell to take the blame. Let the international authorities and homeland security and everyone else go after them and end it there. But…I couldn't be sure what your father had told you, what Dibianu might have blabbed tonight."

Abigail didn't react. She wouldn't shiver in front of this man. But she would fight until the end. "Did you leave all of your guests for me, Mr. Benison? I'm touched."

His chuckle cackled with a trace of disapproval. "Don't flatter yourself, my dear. I rushed out of the house to help with the search for you. But…alas…no one will find you. Your knight in shining armor couldn't protect you, no matter how hard he tried."

Panic hit Abigail with a cold slap. "What did you do to him?"

"He's alive. In the hospital with a serious concussion. That'll keep him away for a few days and if it doesn't… well… And in the meantime…you and I have some business to finish."

"What do you want?" she asked, her prayers centered on Dylan and his safety, her mind whirling with what had been there in front of her all along. This man had controlled her father's holdings, his investments and… his will.

Benison leaned down and lifted her so hard, her dress ripped at the waist. "I want you to die," he said with a cold indifference. "I never expected you to return to that old farmhouse, but you did. We had to come up with a plan to get you to leave again but then…that stupid little bodyguard Dibianu found out the truth and planned to warn you before I could…dispose of you."

Omar Dibianu had been her father's bodyguard. It

made perfect sense now. And he'd been so devoted he'd risked his life to save her, too.

Benison was behind all of this. She stared at the emblem on his cuff link. The letters *OBD* carved in a filigree setting. Orson D. Benison? She'd seen that same emblem somewhere.

"You killed my father?"

"I had him killed," Benison said. "A tragedy but… you see, we needed your land. We need more land for our cause."

"What cause?" Abigail said, tears falling down her face. "My father was always kind to you in spite of your difference of opinion on this country. He trusted you to take care of things. Why would you kill him for our land?"

"He was getting too close," Benison said, his face inches from hers. "He found information that would have exposed the Order of Destiny. I had no choice. And I have no choice with you, Abigail. That house you love so much? It's on fire. Burning right now. With no close relatives, the land will revert back to me, per your father's last wishes."

Order of Destiny. OBD. Poppy! Poppy had been wearing a medallion with the same initials on it. The *O* and the *D* with a swirling *B* in between.

Abigail didn't let on. "I don't believe you'd burn down my home and my father wouldn't leave anything to you."

"I had someone else set the fire. Your dear Poppy Sutton reluctantly put a torch to the place. She had to kill your nosy little assistant since Poppy's carelessness is what made your father suspicious. And then CiCi asked Poppy about some papers she found in your office— papers I'm sure your savvy father left there for you. She wanted to show them to you and we couldn't let her do that. You inherited everything but you'll be dead and since I managed to set up a provision in the will, we can slowly work toward taking over the land. For our cause."

Abigail glanced around, frantic to see her home again. "You can't burn down my home."

"Don't believe me?" He yanked her arm, causing her to scream out in pain. "Come and see, dear girl."

He shoved her toward a boarded window and slammed it open. "Look to the west, over the tree line."

Abigail could see the brightly lit horizon, see the flames shooting up in the night sky. She screamed, twisted against his clammy grip. "Let me go. Why would Poppy set my house on fire?"

"Because she's one of us," Benison said with a soft smile. "We're building an empire, an army that will take back what this country has lost. But we need more land for training and housing. We need your land, Abigail."

He held her there at the window, with the cold wind blowing over her while she watched the flames growing into a white-gold arc. "We own close to five hundred acres that connect to your place but we need more land to train an army and you're the only person standing in our way."

SIXTEEN

Dylan found Tico at headquarters and opened the back hatch to let the eager dog inside. "C'mon, boy. We gotta find her."

He had Abigail's scent on his clothes, that sweet floral scent that only reminded him of her goodness. Tico smelled it, too. They'd find her.

He'd managed to get dressed and out of the hospital before anyone else could stop him. His head throbbed and his vision was still dotted with black spots but he wasn't going to lie there and let them kill her.

Because in spite of his concussion, he'd seen something that jarred him into action before he'd passed out.

A limo had pulled up at the crash scene. Dylan remembered trying to get to Abigail, trying to call her name. The limo door had opened and he'd seen...Orson Benison sitting there.

Then he'd passed out. Had the lawyer come to help? Or had he kidnapped Abigail to make sure she never talked to anyone again?

Dylan had come back to the farm on a hunch after hearing the captain outside his room shouting orders into his phone. He figured the snipers had a hideout nearby and now he saw the smoke and flames when he reached the end of the lane to the Wheaton farm. Abigail! Dylan's pulse hammered in his ear and a wave of dizziness hit him. He stopped the vehicle and let Tico out, then both of them ran toward the flames.

When Dylan made it to the yard, a tall form came toward him. Captain McCord. "Ralsey, what are you doing here?"

"I have to get to her," Dylan said. "I have to—"

The captain held him. "Listen to me. Listen. As far as we can tell, no one is in the house."

Dylan gulped a breath, blinked. "But you don't know."

"We have new information," the captain shouted over the sounds of sirens and firemen running back and forth. "The farm next door. We traced one of the IP addresses back to that location. Dylan, we think they might be holding her there."

"*He's* holding her there," Dylan shouted. "It's Orson Benison, sir."

Abigail stared up at the man who had presented himself as a Washington icon. Rich, powerful, concerned, caring. And evil.

The Order of Destiny hoped to change the country. A vigilante fringe element that had the backing of some very powerful silent partners. And her sweet, trusting father had somehow stumbled on the truth so…they'd killed him. And they'd killed everyone else who'd found little clues of their actions—CiCi and Omar—and now they'd kill Abigail.

But they had underestimated the strength of a Wheaton.

She sat listening to Benison's elaborate explanations and realized she was being held by a psychopath of the worst kind.

"Why didn't you kill me at the wreck site?" she asked now, trying to stall him.

He shook his head. "We tried. Had to get out of there so we took you." He leaned close again, his cold eyes moving over her face. "So I could make you see, give you one last chance to come to our side."

Abigail's laughter echoed over the freezing cold barn. "I'd rather die."

"Okay then."

He jerked her up out of the chair and dragged her toward the back of the barn. "The stream will carry your body back toward your home. This unrelenting faction kidnapped you and brought you to your home and set fire to it. But you managed to get out. Only with the snow and cold, you grew disoriented and fell in the river."

Abigail closed her eyes to the chilling image. "And what is your excuse?"

"Me, I'll make it back to the city and my party, where I'll explain that you've been taken and I'll put on a sad, forlorn face."

She got the picture. "And after a few months, you'll disclose the addendum to the will and you'll take over my land."

"Yes, all perfectly legal and indisputable."

And forged.

She searched for something, anything, to stop him. When he pushed open an old door, the blinding snow hit her like a wet, tattered blanket and she knew she had to make a break and run. She looked down at her dress and realized she was still wearing her sparkling dress shoes. He had her outside now, tugging and pushing her toward the sound of the cold, flowing water. Abigail held back, waiting for her chance.

And then as they stumbled over a rocky incline, she

gathered her strength and lifted her three-inch shoe heel and slammed it down on the instep of his right foot, wedging the slender stiletto heel inside his shoe laces.

And then she dug in her heel while Benison screamed in agony.

After that, everything seemed to shift. She heard angry barking off in the distance, heard someone calling her name.

Dylan and Tico! They'd found her.

Benison slapped at her, his shocked expression etched in pain. He grabbed her close. "Goodbye, Abigail."

She waited, praying, as he pushed her up over the bluff, his hands on her waist. But before he gave her a final shove down into the rocky stream, a furry ball of pure rage lunged out of the woods.

Abigail screamed and fell back, hitting the rocks, while Benison turned and put his hands over his face. Tico knocked him hard against the aged roots and jagged boulders and sank his teeth into one of Benison's arms. The old man curled in a ball and cried out.

But…no one was listening.

Abigail looked up and saw Dylan, still in his dirty, torn tux. He reached down and lifted her up and without a word, he untied her hands and then he took her into his arms and held her shivering body against the solid warmth of his chest and wrapped his tuxedo jacket around her.

"I love you," he said against her hair.

"I love you, too."

Christmas Day

Abigail turned to admire the Christmas tree once again. It was a small tree, in a two-story row house in a quiet Brooklyn neighborhood. And it was the most beautiful tree she'd ever seen.

Because Dylan was standing there beside her.

His mother was in the kitchen creating some good-smelling dishes for their Christmas dinner and his father was in the small, comfortable den watching *It's a Wonderful Life.*

Dylan pulled her into his arms. "So...how does this work? You'll repair the farmhouse first?"

She nodded, touched. He still wasn't sure about this but he was willing to try. "Yes. The snow and the built-in sprinkler system that Sam installed saved the house, but the kitchen and garage will have to be rebuilt. Poppy might be a criminal but she didn't want to burn down that house while she was in her own quarters. I'm so thankful Louie was there and called the local fire department."

"Me, too," Dylan said. "Then the captain and my team showed up after finding out about your neighbors. I heard him shouting orders at the hospital after he got the report." He touched a hand to the bandage on her forehead. "I was so afraid you were in that house."

"You found me," Abigail replied. "That's all that matters."

"It's over." He kissed her there by the tree. "We've taken a lot of them into custody and the rest are scattered and fractured. Benison can't buy his way out of this one. You're safe now."

Abigail looked over at him. "And what about you, Dylan? Do you finally feel safe enough to trust me?"

He looked flustered and then he smiled. "I brought you home to meet my parents. What do you think?"

Abigail laughed and held him close. "I think I've finally come home, too. Merry Christmas."

"Merry Christmas," he said, his hand on her cheek.

The fire crackled a new kind of warmth while the snow-covered world surrounded them in a white cocoon of hope.

Then they felt a nudge at their feet. Tico, trying to get in on this. "I love you, too," she said to the big dog. "Merry Christmas, Tico."

Tico woofed in agreement and then did a circle in front of the fire. Abigail took in the sweet scene of the dog, the fire and the tree. Then she kissed her holiday hero.

* * * * *

Dear Reader,

I am happy to be a part of this two-in-one with my friend
Shirlee McCoy. It's always fun to take secondary characters and tell their stories, and that is what I did with
Dylan Ralsey. His profile intrigued me, and I wanted to
give him a strong, interesting heroine who could make
him see his worth. Abigail seemed to fit the bill. These
two characters had a lot to work through since they came
from different backgrounds. But they made it through. I
hope you enjoyed this story, and I'm wishing you a wonderful Christmas season and the best New Year!

Until next time, may the angels watch over you. Always.

Lenora Worth

Fiona said she'd crack them sooner or later. But the techs had picked up a pattern that was disturbing.

Omar Dibianu followed Abigail's blog and lurked on almost a daily basis on her website. Now he'd become more bold, sending her that text in such an urgent manner. Could he be part of the faction behind these attempts on her life?

"What if we're taking her right into a trap?" he asked the captain after they'd established that they didn't have any other solid leads.

"The man would be foolish to try anything tonight," Captain McCord replied. "We've swept the venue every hour on the hour and we'll keep doing that right up to and during the event. We'll have eyes on everyone entering and leaving the place and you'll have eyes on our subject. At best, we'll be able to corner the man and ask him a few questions."

"And the worst?" Dylan asked, knowing the answer.

"The worst is that an attempt is made and we get her out of there and capture her assailant all in one fell swoop."

"I don't like it," Dylan admitted. "I shouldn't have let her talk me into this."

"She wanted to come and we all made sure it was her decision." The captain glanced at his watch. "You need to go get all fancied up. Be aware and be careful, got it?"

"Got it," Dylan replied. He'd be on hyperalert the whole night.

Four hours later, Abigail stood in front of a full-length mirror, wearing a royal blue empire-style dress with sheer capped sleeves and a sheer bodice embroidered with tiny white pearls and crystals. CiCi had helped her pick it out at a very upscale shop in Paris weeks ago.

Her assistant had sent her holiday clothes to the farm, knowing Abigail would eventually go back there.

The festive dress and her mother's diamond stud earrings should cheer Abigail but she only felt defeated and gloomy. Her father had always looked dashing and gentlemanly in a tuxedo.

Dabbing at her eyes, she had a moment of panic. Maybe going to this big event so soon after her father's death was a bad idea. But she'd made the decision and she'd stick to it. Get in, make the connection and get out.

That was Dylan's motto. He'd told her they'd go in and mingle, let her connect with the very anxious Mr. Omar Dibianu and see what he had to offer and then they'd get her out of there.

"You can do this," she whispered to her reflection. "You have on a good concealer, after all."

Her mother used to say a good concealer underneath the eyes could hide a multitude of problems.

I need more than a concealer, Mother. I need you and Daddy back.

Abigail touched a hand to the shimmering bodice of her dress. She knew her parents were in her heart so that gave her the courage and comfort she needed to make this one bold move.

When a knock came at her door at precisely seven o'clock, she knew it had to be Dylan. The man was very punctual.

"How do I look?" she whispered to Tico. The big dog gave her an approving doggy smile.

She took a calming breath, checked herself in the mirror and asked who was there.

"Dylan," he said.

Abigail opened the door and lost her heart.

Dylan in a tuxedo, his black hair glistening and curling around his forehead and ears, his eyes inky and wide open. And on her.

He did a thorough sweep, taking in her dress before his gaze came back to her face. "Are…are you ready?"

She nodded, unable to speak, unable to move.

"You'll need a wrap."

She whirled to get her white wool evening cloak and her matching clutch. When she turned around, Dylan was there. He took the wrap and put it over her shoulders, his hands lingering near her neck.

"You look amazing," he said, his breath warm on her ear.

Abigail closed her eyes and willed herself to remain aloof and unaffected. But oh, she was affected. She was shaken and moved and changed and…she was falling for a man who didn't want someone like her in his life. A man who had decided he couldn't afford to have someone to love.

"Abigail…"

For a brief moment, she felt as if he needed to say something more, something personal and intimate. But he held her, his hands warm on her skin.

"Let's go," he said, shifting away.

Abigail turned and nodded, regaining her balance. "This should be an interesting evening."

He gave her one of those silky black Dylan stares, his hand touching her elbow. "You can say that again."

FOURTEEN

The big white mansion shined like a jewel in a neighborhood near DuPont Circle, and tonight one of Washington's finest historical homes was all decked out for the holiday season. But the decorations were subtle and understated. An evergreen wreath trimmed in red ribbons hung on each of the impressive floor-to-ceiling windows on all levels of the home and two huge matching wreaths graced the beveled glass doors. Candelabras stood lit with white candles on each side of the entryway and a huge tree that could be seen through the lower level windows offered a welcoming sight.

Abigail had been here before many times so she knew the history of the Benison Mansion. Orson D. Benison owned a thriving law firm that had been in his family for generations and while he'd inherited most of his wealth, he'd accumulated even more through solid investments and buying into a couple of internet start-up companies. He had helped her father with his investments, too.

He also controlled politicians on both sides of the aisle and represented the crooked ones who were willing to pay a hefty sum to use his services. Her father had not particularly cared for Mr. Benison's boastful attitude but he'd always accepted invitations to events here as a courtesy